Thomas Middleton and William Rowley's
The Changeling: A Retelling

David Bruce

Published by David Bruce, 2023.

THOMAS MIDDLETON AND WILLIAM ROWLEY'S THE CHANGELING: A RETELLING

First edition. February 25, 2023.

ISBN: 979-8215331903

Written by David Bruce.

Table of Contents

Dedication

DEDICATED TO MY SISTER ROSA

The Doing of Good Deeds is Important

As a free person, you can choose to live your life as a good person or as a bad person. To be a good person, do good deeds. To be a bad person, do bad deeds. If you do good deeds, you will become good. If you do bad deeds, you will become bad. To become the person you want to be, act as if you already are that kind of person. Each of us chooses what kind of person we will become. To become a good person, do the things a good person does. To become a bad person, do the things a bad person does. The opportunity to take action to become the kind of person you want to be is yours.

"I Will Go with You Into the Grave"

In a medieval Christian mystery play, a man asks who will go with him into the grave when he dies and give him support at the Day of Judgment. Time after time, he hears the answer, "I won't go with you into the grave." His wife won't go with him into the grave, his children won't go with him into the grave, his priest won't go with him into the grave, his friends won't go with him into the grave — even his wealth won't go with him into the grave. Finally, the man's good deeds say, "I will go with you into the grave," and the man and his good deeds knock at the door of death, together. Your good deeds will plead for you on the Day of Judgment.

"Do Small Kindnesses for People"

Amy Alkon, aka "The Advice Goddess," does good deeds, as well as write an advice column for alternative newspapers. She advises, "Do small kindnesses for people." For example, she buys and reads a newspaper every day. When she is finished reading it, she will look around wherever she is — often, she is in a café — and often see somebody who is looking for a newspaper. She will then ask, "Sir, would you like my newspaper?" She points out, "You've noticed a stranger, you've solved their problem, you've gone out of your way to do it, and they're gonna feel very good about that, and I think people will tend to pass on good deeds, do other good deeds, if you do good deeds for them." She adds that "it does make a difference."

"Dear"

One of the things that Kurt Vonnegut, Jr., believes firmly is this: "God d*mn it, you've got to be kind." One of the things that cheers him up is buying a morning cup of coffee in New York City, which he describes as mad for money. He says, "You can go into a little café and the waitress calls you 'dear' even though she knows the bill will be a small expenditure and the tip tiny. So she is responding to you as a person and feels happy and wants to communicate."

Show the Haters that They are Wrong

Robert DeMott and Dave Smith became friends in the early 1970s. They had a number of things in common that facilitated their friendship: they were or would become editors, scholars, teachers, and writers, plus both had been told as undergraduates by professors that they "were not smart enough or able enough to amount to much in the 'real' world" — predictions that they ignored. Mr. DeMott became a noted John Steinbeck scholar, and Mr. Smith became a noted poet.

Educate Yourself
Read Like A Wolf Eats
Be Excellent to Each Other
Books Then, Books Now, Books Forever

***

In this retelling, as in all my retellings, I have tried to make the work of literature accessible to modern readers who may lack some of the knowledge about mythology, religion, and history that the literary work's contemporary audience had.

Do you know a language other than English? If you do, I give you permission to translate this book, copyright your translation, publish or self-publish it, and keep all the royalties for yourself. (Do give me credit, of course, for the original retelling.)

I would like to see my retellings of classic literature used in schools, so I give permission to the country of Finland (and all other countries) to give copies of any or all of my retellings to all students forever. I also give permission to the state of Texas (and all other states) to give copies of any or all of my retellings to all students forever. I also give permission to all teachers to give copies of any or all of my retellings to all students forever. Of course, libraries are welcome to use my eBooks for free.

Teachers need not actually teach my retellings. Teachers are welcome to give students copies of my eBooks as background material. For example, if they are teaching Homer's *Iliad* and *Odyssey*, teachers are welcome to give students copies of my *Virgil's* Aeneid: *A Retelling in Prose* and tell them, "Here's another ancient epic you may want to read in your spare time."

CAST OF CHARACTERS

Male Characters

VERMANDERO, father to Beatrice. Governor of the castle of Alicante.

TOMAZO de Piracquo, a noble lord.

ALONZO de Piracquo, his brother, suitor to Beatrice.

ALSEMERO, a nobleman, suitor to Beatrice.

JASPERINO, his friend.

ALIBIUS, a jealous doctor.

LOLLIO, his serving-man.

PEDRO, friend to Antonio.

ANTONIO, the fool.

FRANCISCUS, the madman.

DEFLORES, servant to Vermandero. "Deflores" suggests "deflower." Deflores is a gentleman in social rank.

MADMEN and FOOLS.

Two SERVANTS to Alsemero.

A SERVANT to Vermandero.

Female Characters

BEATRICE, also called JOANNA or BEATRICE JOANNA, daughter to Vermandero.

DIAPHANTA, her waiting-woman.

ISABELLA, wife to Alibius.

The Scene: ALICANTE, a port on the east coast of Spain.

NOTES:

A changeling can be:

1) A person who changes or is changed.

2) A person who is changeable.

3) A person substituted secretly for another.

4) A simpleton.

5) A person who is exchanged for another. Fairies were supposed to sometimes exchange an ugly infant of theirs for a good-looking human infant.

As will become clear, many characters in *The Changeling* have either changed themselves in some way or have been substituted for another person.

In this society, a person of higher rank would use "thou," "thee," "thine," and "thy" when referring to a person of lower rank. (These terms were also used affectionately and between equals.) A person of lower rank would use "you" and "your" when referring to a person of higher rank.

"Sirrah" was a title used to address someone of a social rank inferior to the speaker. Friends, however, could use it to refer to each other.

The word "wench" at this time was not necessarily negative. It was often used affectionately.

Scholars believe that Middleton wrote the main plot (Beatrice, Deflores, Alsemero, Alonzo), while Rowley wrote the subplot (Alibius, Isabella, Antonio, Franciscus).

CHAPTER 1

— 1.1 —

On a street near the harbor of Alicante, a port on the east coast of Spain, Alsemero, a nobleman, was in love. He was supposed to set sail for Malta, but he had fallen in love with a woman named Beatrice.

Alsemero said to himself:

"It was in the temple — the church — where I first saw her, and now again I saw her there. What omen yet follows of that? None but imaginary. Why should my hopes or fate be timorous? The place is holy, and so is my intent: I intend marriage to her. I love her beauties to the holy purpose — the sacrament of marriage — and I think that marriage warrants comparison with man's first creation, the blest place, and I think it is his right home back, if he can achieve it."

Adam's job in the Garden of Eden was "*to dress it and keep it*" (Genesis 2:16, King James Version). In other words, Adam's job was to cultivate the garden.

According to Alsemero, marriage is the Garden of Eden: the Earthly Paradise. A man in a good marriage will be happy.

Alsemero continued speaking to himself:

"The church has first begun our interview — our mutual view of each other — and that's the place that must join us into one, so there's beginning and perfection, too."

The church was where he first saw Beatrice, and the church would be where he would marry her if he could convince her to accept him as her husband.

A circle symbolizes perfection.

A vagina can be regarded as a circle. If a marriage happened, the church would make Alsemero and Beatrice husband and wife: a married couple — one out of two.

Jasperino, Alsemero's friend, entered the scene.

"O sir, are you here?" Jasperino said. "Come, the wind's fair for your voyage. You are likely to have a swift and pleasant passage."

Alsemero was supposed to go on a voyage, but his falling in love had made him not want to go.

"Surely you are deceived, friend," Alsemero said. "The wind is contrary in my best judgment."

For him to set off on the voyage, the wind had to be blowing in the right direction. In fact, the wind was blowing in the right direction for travel to Malta, but Alsemero did not want to admit that.

He wanted to stay in the port city of Alicante and court Beatrice, so yes, the wind was contrary to the way he wanted it to be.

"What, for Malta?" Jasperino said. "If you could buy a gale among the witches, they could not serve you such a lucky pennyworth — such a bargain — as comes in God's name."

In this society, witches were believed to exist and to be able to cause storms at sea.

The fair weather had come in God's name: freely, without charge, and naturally.

"Just now I observed the temple's weather-vane to turn full in my face," Alsemero said. "I know the wind is against me."

"Against you?" Jasperino said. "Then you don't know where you are."

"Not well indeed," Alsemero said.

"Are you not well, sir?" Jasperino asked.

"Yes, I am well, Jasperino, unless there is some hidden malady within me that I don't understand," Alsemero said.

Jasperino said:

"And that I begin to fear, sir. Until now, I never knew your inclination for travels to be at a pause no matter what cause arose to hinder it.

"Ashore you were accustomed to call up your servants and help to harness your horses for a speedy departure.

"At sea I have seen you weigh the anchor with the sailors, hoist sails for fear of losing the foremost breath, be in continual prayers for fair winds — and have you changed your prayers? Have you changed what you pray for?"

To weigh anchor means to raise the anchor from the sea floor so the ship can sail.

"No, friend, I keep the same church, the same devotion," Alsemero said.

He kept the same love for Beatrice.

Jasperino said:

"I'm sure you are not a lover. The Stoic was found in you long ago."

A Stoic is able to suppress emotions.

Jasperino continued:

"Neither your mother nor your best friends, who have set snares of beauty, aye, and choice ones, too, could ever trap you that way."

They could not entice Alsemero to fall in love and marry.

Jasperino continued:

"What might be the cause of your disinclination to travel?"

"Lord, how violent thou are," Alsemero said. "I was only meditating about something I heard within the temple."

That would be something said by Beatrice.

"Is this violence?" Jasperino said. "It is only idleness compared with your haste yesterday."

Yesterday, Alsemero had been eager to go to Malta. That was before he had seen Beatrice.

"I'm all this while going, man," Alsemero said.

Two of Alsemero's servants entered the scene.

"You are going backwards, I think, sir," Jasperino said. "Look, your servants have come here."

"The seamen call," the first servant said. "Shall we put your trunks on board?"

"No, not today," Alsemero said.

"It is the critical — the astrologically crucial — day, it seems," Jasperino said, "and the sign is in Aquarius."

The constellation Aquarius is the Water-Carrier.

Astrologically speaking, when the Sun is in Aquarius, it is a good time for a sea voyage.

"We must not go to sea today," the second servant whispered to the first servant. "This smoke will bring forth fire."

A proverb stated, "Where there's smoke, there's fire."

The smoke was Alsemero's concealed love for Beatrice. Servants know much about their masters.

Alsemero said:

"Keep everything on shore.

"I do not know the end, yet, of an affair I have in hand and must complete before I can go to sea."

"Well, whatever is your pleasure," the first servant said.

"Let him just take his leisure, too," the second servant whispered to the first servant. "We are safer on land."

Sailing can be dangerous.

Alsemero's two servants exited.

Beatrice, Diaphanta, and some servants entered the scene. Diaphanta was Beatrice's waiting-woman.

Alsemero bowed to Beatrice and kissed her.

Jasperino said to himself:

"What is this now! The laws of the Medes are changed, surely."

The laws of the Medes were reputed to never change.

Daniel 6:8 states, "*Now, O king, establish the decree, and sign the writing, that it be not changed, according to the law of the Medes and Persians, which altereth not*" (King James Version).

Jasperino continued saying to himself:

"Greet a woman! He kisses, too! Wonderful! Where did he learn this? And he does it perfectly, too; on my word, he never rehearsed it before.

"Nay, go on, this will be stranger and better news at Valencia than if he had ransomed half of Greece from the Turk!"

Valencia was another seaport on the east coast of Spain. Alsemero was born at Valencia, which is approximately 75 miles north of Alicante.

From 1460 to 1830, which includes the time in which this book is set (early 1600s), Greece was part of the Ottoman Empire.

"You are a scholar, sir," Beatrice said.

"A weak one, lady," Alsemero said.

"Which of the sciences is this love you speak of?" Beatrice asked.

In this society, "sciences" means branches of knowledge, but not necessarily scientific knowledge.

"From your tongue I take it to be music," Alsemero said.

"You are skillful in it, you who can sing at first sight," Beatrice said.

"Sing at first sight" can mean 1) sight-read music, and/or 2) fall in love at first sight and confess that love.

"And I have showed you all my skill at once," Alsemero said. "I want more words to express me further and must be forced to repetition: I love you dearly."

Beatrice said:

"Be better advised, sir.

"Our eyes are sentinels unto our judgments, and they should give certain judgment what they see. But they are rash sometimes and tell us wonders about common things, which when our judgments find the errors out, our judgments can then rebuke the eyes, and call them blind."

Many men have fallen temporarily in love because of beer goggles. When drunk, they have been attracted to a woman, but when they are sober again, they are no longer attracted to her.

Alsemero said:

"But I am at a further stage than that, lady. I am past that point.

"Yesterday was my eyes' employment — I used my eyes — and now they have brought my judgment to here, where both sight and judgment are agreed."

Alsemero said:

"Both houses then consenting, it is agreed, there lacks only the confirmation by the hand royal — that's your part, lady."

"Both houses" was word play on the Houses of Parliament — the House of Lords and the House of Commons — which here represent sight and judgment.

The royal signature was needed for a bill to become law.

Alsemero's eyes and judgment had agreed that they loved Beatrice; now Beatrice's agreement to love Alsemero was needed.

Beatrice said:

"Oh, there's one above me, sir."

Her father had some authority over her. So did God.

Beatrice said to herself:

"If only the past five days could be recalled! Surely, my eyes were mistaken; this is the man who was meant for me. That he should come so near his time, and miss it!"

Five days earlier, Beatrice had agreed to marry Alonzo de Piracquo.

Her father — one above her — wanted her to marry Alonzo de Piracquo.

Jasperino said to himself:

"We might have come by the carriers — land transport — from Valencia, I see, and saved all our sea-provision. We are at the farthest part of our journey, surely."

Jasperino was afraid that Alsemero would not go to Malta but would continue to remain in Alicante. He had gone as far as he would go.

Jasperino continued speaking to himself:

"I think I should do something, too; I meant to be a venturer — an investor — in this voyage."

"Yonder's another vessel. I'll board her; if she is a lawful prize, down goes her topsail!"

Pirates could lawfully prey on certain ships: enemies of the pirates' king. A ship would lower its topsail as a sign of surrender.

But this vessel was the weaker vessel: Diaphanta, Beatrice's waiting-woman.

1 Peter 3:7 states, "*Likewise, ye husbands, dwell with them according to knowledge, giving honour unto the wife, as unto the weaker vessel, and as being heirs together of the grace of life; that your prayers be not hindered*" (King James Version).

Jasperino may regard an unmarried woman as a lawful prize.

Her upper sail would be her bodice.

Jasperino wanted to "board" — get on top of — Diaphanta.

He moved over to her so he could talk to her.

Deflores entered the scene. He was a servant to Vermandero, Beatrice's father.

Deflores had a skin condition that made him ugly. Beatrice intensely disliked him.

Deflores began, "Lady, your father—"

Beatrice rudely interrupted, "— is in health, I hope."

"Your eye shall instantly instruct you, lady," Deflores said. "He's coming hitherward."

Beatrice said:

"What was the need then for your duteous preface? I had rather he had come unexpected; you must stall a good presence with unnecessary blabbing."

"Stall" can mean 1) forestall, and 2) make stale.

Her father had a "good pretense": He was an impressive-looking man.

Beatrice continued:

"And how welcome for your part you are, I'm sure you know."

Deflores said to himself:

"Will it never mend, this scorn, one way or the other? Must I be commanded to follow continually while she flies away from me?"

The scorn could be mended if Beatrice ceased to scorn him, or if Deflores ceased to expose himself to her scorn.

The Fates — or Deflores' lust — were commanding Deflores to pursue Beatrice.

Deflores continued saying to himself:

"Well, Fates, do your worst, I'll please myself with the sight of her, at all opportunities, if only to spite her anger."

The three Fates are ancient goddesses who commanded the pulse of life; they controlled human life. Clotho spun the thread of life. Lachesis measured the thread of life, determining how long a person lived. Atropos cut the thread of life; when the thread was cut, the person died.

Deflores continued saying to himself:

"I know that Beatrice would rather see me dead than living, and yet she knows no cause for it but a peevish will."

"You seemed displeased, lady, suddenly," Alsemero said.

Beatrice replied:

"I beg your pardon, sir, it is my infirmity, nor can I give any other reason than any other person — man or woman — could give about some particular thing they must reject as if it were a deadly poison, although that particular thing would be wholesome to a thousand other tastes.

"Such to my eyes is that same fellow there: Deflores. To me he is the same that is reported of the basilisk."

A basilisk is a mythological monster that could kill people simply by looking at them.

Alsemero replied:

"This is a frequent frailty in our nature. There's scarcely a man among a thousand who is both healthy and lacks a personal quirk: Most men are healthy, but they are imperfect.

"One dislikes the scent of roses, which to infinite numbers of people is very pleasing and sweet-smelling.

"One dislikes medicinal oil that is the enemy of poison.

Castor oil was used as a purgative.

Alsemero continued:

"Another dislikes wine, the cheerer of the heart, and the lively refresher of the countenance."

Psalm 104:15 states, *"And wine that maketh glad the heart of man, and oil to make his face to shine, and bread which strengtheneth man's heart"* (King James Version).

Alsemero continued:

"Indeed, this fault, if it is a fault, is general: There's scarcely a thing but it is both loved and loathed.

"I, myself, I must confess, have the same frailty."

"And what may be your poison, sir?" Beatrice asked. "To ask you that is bold, but I will ask you."

"My poison is what might be your desire perhaps, a cherry," Alsemero answered.

A proverb stated, "One man's meat [food] is another man's poison."

"I am no enemy to any creature that my memory has stored in my mind except yonder gentleman," Beatrice said.

"He does ill to tempt your sight, if he knew it," Alsemero said.

In other words: If he knows that you dislike him, he ought to stay out of your sight.

"He cannot be ignorant of that, sir," Beatrice said. "I have not spared to tell him so, and I lack means to help myself, since he's a gentleman in good standing with my father and follows him as a servant."

Beatrice's father liked Deflores and employed him as a servant.

"He's out of his place then now," Alsemero said.

In other words: He should stay away from you, and he is not behaving the way that a servant ought to behave.

They continued talking off to the side, while Jasperino talked to Diaphanta, Beatrice's waiting-woman.

"I am a mad wag, wench," Jasperino said.

He meant that he was high-spirited, but Diaphanta deliberately misinterpreted "mad" as meaning "insane."

"So I think, but for your comfort I can tell you we have a doctor in the city who undertakes the cure of such," Diaphanta said.

That doctor's name is Alibius.

"Bah, I know what medicine is best for the state of my own body," Jasperino said.

"It is scarcely a well-governed state, I believe," Diaphanta said.

"I could show thee such a thing with an ingredient that we two would compound together, and if it did not tame the maddest blood in the town for two hours afterward, I'll never profess doctoring again," Jasperino said.

Jasperino wanted to show her a "thing" with an ingredient: The thing is a penis.

An ingredient could be pounded with a mortar and pestle, but Jasperino meant a man and a woman having a session of sexual pounding. Together, they would make an ingredient: semen. In the "mortar," semen and a woman's vaginal lubrication would be mixed and compounded.

A penis that has ejaculated usually becomes a tame penis for two hours afterward.

"Com" in "compounding" means "with" or "together."

"Com" is close in pronunciation to "cum," which meant then what it means now.

"A little poppy, sir, would be good to cause you to sleep," Diaphanta said.

"Poppy" is opium.

Jasperino said:

"Poppy! I'll give thee a pop in the lips for that first, and begin there."

In this context, a "pop" is a noisy kiss. But another meaning is a thrust in the lips of a vulva.

Jasperino kissed Diaphanta.

He began with the lips of Diaphanta's face, but he hoped to move to different lips that belonged to her.

Poppy can make one sleep, and so can a vigorous session of sex.

Jasperino then said:

'Poppy is one simple — a medicinal herb — indeed, and cuckoo, what you call it, is another."

The cuckoo-pint, aka wild arum, is a phallic-shaped plant.

The ladies' smock is another variety of cuckoo flower; it was regarded as a cure for madness.

Jasperino concluded:

"I'll discover no more now; another time I'll show thee all."

"Discover" means 1) reveal, and 2) lay bare (literally).

Vermandero, Beatrice's father, entered the scene, accompanied by some servants. Vermandero was the Governor of the castle of Alicante.

"My father, sir," Beatrice said to Alsemero.

"Oh, Joanna, I came to meet thee," Vermandero said. "Your devotion's ended?"

Joanna is Beatrice's other name. She is Beatrice Joanna.

By "devotion," Vermandero meant "act of worship."

The church service had ended, but so had Beatrice's devotion to her betrothed.

Beatrice said:

"For this time, sir."

She then said to herself:

"I shall change my saint, I am afraid. I find a giddy turning in me."

"Giddy turning" cam mean 1) dizzying vertigo, or 2) insane conversion.

She would exchange her Heavenly saint for an Earthly saint: Alsemero.

She then said out loud:

"Sir, for this while I am beholden and indebted to this gentleman who left his own way to keep me company, and in discourse I find him much desiring to see your castle.

"He has deserved it, sir, if you please to grant it."

Vermandero said to Alsemero:

"With all my heart, sir.

"Yet there's a pre-condition. I must know your country. We are not accustomed to give a survey of our chief strengths — chief fortresses — to strangers. Our citadels are placed conspicuous to outward view on the tops of promontories, but within are secrets."

Some of the people within also have secrets.

"I am a Valencian, sir," Alsemero said.

Vermandero said:

"A Valencian? That's native to this region of Spain, sir."

Alicante and Valencia were about 75 miles apart.

Vermandero then asked:

"What is your name, please?"

"My name is Alsemero, sir," he replied.

"Alsemero?" Vermandero said. "You are not the son of John de Alsemero, are you?"

"The same, sir," Alsemero said.

"My best love bids you welcome," Vermandero said.

Beatrice said to herself, "My father was accustomed to call me his best love, and if he means that *I* bid Alsemero welcome, then he speaks a most unfeigned truth."

Vermandero said:

"Oh, sir, I knew your father. We two were acquainted long ago, before our chins were worth iulan down, and so we continued to be acquaintances until the stamp of time had coined us into silver — that is, until time gave us grey beards."

"Iulan down" is the first growth of beard. The Greek word *ioulos* means "first growth of beard."

Vermandero then said:

"Well, he's gone; a good soldier went with him."

"You went together in that, sir," Alsemero said.

Alsemero meant that Vermandero was as good a soldier as Alsemero's father.

Vermandero said:

"No, by Saint Jacques, I came behind him. Yet I have done some deeds, too. An unhappy day swallowed him at last at Gibraltar in fight with those rebellious Hollanders. Isn't that so?"

The brother of John the Apostle, Saint Jacques is the patron saint of Spain. He is also known as Saint James the Greater, aka Saint James of Compostella. He is also called Santiago.

At this time, the Netherlands were under the dominion of Spain. On 25 April 1607, the Netherlands defeated Spain in the Battle of Gibraltar.

Alsemero said, "I would have revenged my father's death, or followed him in fated death, had not the recent league prevented me."

On 8 April 1609, the Netherlands and Spain signed the Treaty of the Hague, which began a twelve-year truce from 1609 to 1621.

Vermandero said:

"Aye, aye, it was time to breathe: to rest from fighting.

"Oh, Joanna, I should have told thee news: I saw Piracquo lately."

This man was Beatrice Joanna's betrothed: Alonzo de Piracquo.

Beatrice said to herself, "That's ill news."

Vermandero said, "He's hot preparing for this day of triumph. Thou must be a bride within this seven-night: within this week."

"Hot" means eager, and sexually eager.

The day of triumph was the wedding day.

Learning that his beloved, Beatrice, was betrothed, Alsemero grunted.

Beatrice said, "Nay, good sir, be not so violent; with speed I cannot render satisfaction to the dear companion of my soul, virginity, with whom I have lived thus long, and I cannot part with it so rudely and suddenly. Can such friends divide never to meet again without a solemn farewell?"

"Tush, tush, that's a toy: a trifle, a whim," Vermandero said.

Alsemero said to himself:

"I must now part, and never meet again with any joy on earth."

Alsemero said out loud to Vermandero:

"Sir, I beg your pardon. My affairs call on me."

Vermandero said:

"What, sir? What! By no means! You have not changed so soon, I hope?"

Alsemero had previously wanted to see the castle. Had he changed his mind?

Beatrice had made an exchange: in her affections she had exchanged her love for her betrothed for a new love for Alsemero.

Vermandero continued:

"You must see my castle and her best entertainment before we part."

"Entertainment" has a bawdy sense: sexual entertainment.

Vermandero continued:

"I shall think myself unkindly treated otherwise. Come, come, let's go on. I had good hope that you would stay a while with us in Alicante; I might have bid you to my daughter's wedding."

Alsemero said to himself:

"He means to feast me, and he poisons me beforehand."

The "poison" was Beatrice's wedding to another man. Alsemero loved her.

He then said out loud:

"I should be very glad to be there, sir, if my affairs were as I could wish them to be."

"I shall be sorry if you would be not there when it is done, sir, but not so suddenly," Beatrice said.

She did not want a quick wedding.

Vermandero said to Alsemero about Alonzo de Piracquo:

"I tell you, sir, the gentleman's complete — he is everything a gentleman should be. He is a courtier and a gallant, and he is enriched with many fair and noble ornaments: many distinctions.

"I would not exchange him as my son-in-law for any man in Spain, the proudest man, and you should know that we have great ones."

"He's much bound — indebted — to you, sir," Alsemero said.

"He shall be bound — united — to me, as fast as this tie can hold him," Vermandero said. "I'll lack my will — what I want — otherwise."

Beatrice said to herself, "I shall lack my will if you do it: bind him to yourself through marrying him to me."

"Will" can mean "sexual desire."

Vermandero said, "But come, along the way I'll tell you more about him."

Alsemero said to himself, "How shall I dare to venture in his castle when he discharges murderers at the gate? But I must go on, for I cannot go back."

Murderers are small cannon loaded with grapeshot.

By talking about Beatrice's upcoming marriage to Alonzo de Piracquo, Vermandero was metaphorically "murdering" Alsemero.

Looking at Deflores, Beatrice said to herself, "Hasn't this serpent gone yet?"

A serpent appeared in the Garden of Eden and tempted Eve.

She dropped her glove, possibly hoping that Alsemero would pick it up.

Vermandero said to Beatrice:

"Look, girl, thy glove has fallen."

She moved to pick it up, but her father said:

"Wait, wait."

He then said:

"Deflores, help a little."

Deflores picked up the glove, offered it to Beatrice, and said, "Here, lady."

Refusing to take the glove, Beatrice said to him:

"Mischief on your officious forwardness."

In this society, "mischief" is a strong curse. In this society, "mischief means "evil."

Beatrice continued:

"Who bade you to stoop and pick it up?"

Her father had done that.

Beatrice continued:

"These gloves touch my hand no more. There, for the other glove's sake, I part with this glove."

She gave Deflores her other glove and said:

"Take them and take off thine own skin when thou take these gloves off."

Serpents shed their skin.

Deflores had an unsightly skin condition. He may have had a severe and chronic case of acne.

Everyone exited, except Deflores.

Holding the gloves, Deflores said to himself:

"Here's a favor that has come with a mischief."

A favor is a lady's small gift. A lady might give a glove to a knight, who would attach it to his clothing or armor or helmet during a tournament.

Deflores continued talking to himself:

"Now I know that she would prefer to wear my skin tanned in a pair of dancing pumps — dancing shoes — than that I should thrust my fingers into her sockets here."

The sockets were the finger holes in the glove.

Readers may be forgiven for thinking of different kinds of holes.

Deflores continued:

"I know she hates me, yet I cannot choose but love her.

"No matter, if only to vex her, I'll haunt her still. Although I get nothing else, I'll have my will."

"Will" can mean "sexual desire."

Alibius and Lollio talked together in a room in Alibius' madhouse. Lollio was Alibius' serving-man. Alibius was a doctor who took care of madmen; Lollio took care of fools.

"Lollio, I must trust thee with a secret, but thou must keep it secret," Alibius said.

"I was ever close to a secret, sir," Lollio said.

He meant 1) He was always secretive — close-mouthed — about secrets, and 2) He was always close to a private part.

Alibius said:

"The diligence that I have found in thee, the care and industry already past, assures me of thy good continuance.

"Lollio, I have a wife."

He had married Isabella.

"Bah, sir, it is too late to keep her secret," Lollio said. "She's known to be married all the town and country over."

"Too late to keep her secret" means 1) keep her status as a wife secret, and 2) preserve her virginity.

"Married all the town and country over" may hint that she had lovers "all the town and country over."

If so, this would be in Lollio's daydreams.

A clown character, Lollio interpreted "secret" to mean "private parts."

Alibius said:

"Thou go too fast, my Lollio: I acknowledge no man can be barred from knowing that."

He meant knowing that he had a wife.

Alibius continued:

"But there is a knowledge which is nearer, deeper, and sweeter, Lollio."

That "nearer, deeper, and sweeter" knowledge is carnal knowledge.

"Well, sir, let us handle that between you and me," Lollio said.

A bawdy interpretation of Lollio's sentence is that Alibius and Lollio could sexually handle and share Alibius' wife.

Alibius said:

"It is that I am speaking about, man."

He meant handling the problem of keeping an eye on his wife.

Alibius continued:

"Lollio, my wife is young."

"So much the worse to be kept secret, sir," Lollio said.

Lollio meant that she should not be concealed from other men, but Alibius thought that Lollio was saying that since Alibius' wife was young, it would be harder to hide her from other men.

"Why, now thou meet the substance of the point," Alibius said. "I am old, Lollio."

Alibius wanted to conceal his young wife from the sight of young men.

Lollio said, "No, sir. It is I who is 'old Lollio.'"

Alibius said, "Yet why may not this May-December marriage concord and sympathize? Old trees and young plants often grow together, well enough agreeing."

A marriage of young and old can be a happy marriage.

"Aye, sir, but the old trees raise themselves higher and broader than the young plants," Lollio said.

Old trees grow larger, and old cuckolds grow invisible horns on their head.

A cuckold is a man with an unfaithful wife.

Alibius said:

"That's a shrewd application. There's the fear, man.

"I would wear my ring on my own finger. While it is borrowed, it is none of mine, but instead it is his who uses it."

The ring and finger are sexual symbols.

"You must keep it on always then," Lollio said. "If it but lies nearby, one or another will be thrusting into it."

"Thou understand me, Lollio," Alibius said. "Here thy watchful eye must have employment. I cannot always be at home."

In this society, the word "employment" has another meaning: sex.

"I dare swear you cannot," Lollio said.

One meaning of being "at home" is being in his wife's vagina.

"I must look out," Alibius said.

He had to go outside his house once in a while, and he had to look out — take care — to protect himself from being cuckolded.

"I know it," Lollio said. "You must look out: It is every man's case."

One meaning of "case" is "vagina."

"Here I say what thy employment must be," Alibius said. "Thou must watch her treadings, and in my absence supply my place."

"Treadings" can mean 1) movements from one place to another, or 2) sexual movements.

"Supply my place"?

Hmm.

Take Alibius' place in bed?

"I'll do my best, sir," Lollio said. "Yet surely I cannot see whom you should have cause to be jealous — suspicious — of."

"What is thy reason for that, Lollio?" Alibius said. "It is a comfortable — a comforting — question."

It is a question that reassured Alibius.

Lollio said, "We have only two sorts of people in the house, and both are under the whip. Those two sorts of people are fools and madmen. The one has not wit enough to be knaves, and the other has not knavery enough to be fools."

According to Lollio, fools need knavery, and knaves need wit, aka intelligence.

As a doctor, Alibius took care of fools and madmen. The fools were imbeciles.

Alibius said:

"Aye, those are all my patients, Lollio. My profession is the cure of either sort: fools or madmen. My trade, my living it is, I thrive by it.

"But here's the worry that mixes with my profit. Daily visitants come to see my brainsick patients, and I would not have them see my wife. I see gallants who have quick, enticing eyes, who wear rich clothing, and who are very comely and attractive in stature and proportion. These are most shrewd — wicked and difficult to resist — temptations, Lollio."

In this society, an "entertainment" was to look at fools and madmen: inbeciles and insane people.

"They may be easily answered, sir," Lollio said. "If they come to see the fools and madmen, you and I may serve the turn, and let my mistress alone; she's of neither sort."

To "see" someone can have a bawdy meaning: to have sex with.

The daily visitants could "see" Alibius and Lollio; Alibius and Lollio could supply the places of the fools and madmen.

"It is a good ward: a good defensive maneuver," Alibius said. "Indeed, they come to see our madmen or our fools; let them see no more than what they come for. By that reasoning, they must not see her. I'm sure she's no fool."

"And I'm sure she's no madman," Lollio said.

He may have stressed the syllable "man" in "madman."

Alibius said:

"Hold that buckler — that shield — fast, Lollio. Her being neither a fool nor a madman should help protect her. My trust is on thee, and I account it firm and strong.

"What hour is it, Lollio? What time is it?"

"It is close to belly hour, sir," Lollio said.

His stomach was telling him it was almost time to eat.

"Dinner time?" Alibius said. "Thou mean twelve o'clock."

Lollio said, "Yes, sir, for every part has its hour. We wake at six and look about us, that's eye hour; at seven we should pray, that's knee hour; at eight walk, that's leg hour; at nine gather flowers, and pluck a rose, that's nose hour; at ten we drink, that's mouth hour; at eleven search for victuals [food], that's hand hour; at twelve go to dinner, that's belly hour."

"Pluck a rose" can mean "urinate in the garden." In this society, the word "nose" can mean "projecting part," a description that can refer to a penis.

Alibius said:

"You speak profoundly, Lollio; it will be long before all thy 'scholars' learn this lesson, and I did look to have a new 'scholar' entered.

"Wait, I think my expectation has come home. It is being fulfilled."

Pedro and Antonio entered the scene. They were friends.

Antonio was the newest "scholar" to be enrolled in Alibius' "school."

Pedro said to Alibius, "May God save you, sir. My business speaks itself. This sight takes off — removes the need for — the labor of my tongue."

Antonio was wearing clothing that indicated that he was an idiot. He may have been wearing a dunce's hat.

"Aye, aye, sir," Alibius said. "It is plain enough that you mean for him to become my patient."

Pedro gave Alibius money and said, "And if your pains prove to be commodious and beneficial enough to give just some little strength to the sick and weak part of nature in him, these are but patterns — that is, samples — to show you of the whole pieces, aka gold coins, that will follow to you, besides the cost of diet, washing, and other necessaries fully defrayed."

"Believe it, sir, there shall no care be lacking," Alibius said.

"Sir, an officer in this place may deserve something," Lollio said. "The trouble will pass through my hands."

Lollio wanted money, too.

Pedro gave Lollio some money and said, "It is fitting that something should come to your hands then, sir."

Lollio said:

"Yes, sir, it is I who must keep him clean and sweet-smelling, and read to him.

"What is his name?"

"His name is Antonio," Pedro said. "But by the Virgin Mary, we use just half of his name: We call him only Tony."

Lollio said:

"Tony, Tony, it is enough, and a very good name for a fool.

"What's your name, Tony?"

Like a fool, Antonio said, "He, he, he. Well, I thank you, cousin. He, he, he."

Lollio said:

"Good boy, hold up your head.

"He can laugh; I perceive by that he is no beast."

According to Aristotle (*De Partibus Animalium*, III, 10), human beings laugh, and beasts do not laugh.

Pedro said:

"Well, sir, if you can raise him just to any height, any degree of wit, that he might attain, as I might say, just to creep on all fours or walk on crutches towards the chair of wit, it would add an honor to your worthy pains, and a great family might pray for you, a great family to which he should be heir had he discretion to claim and guide and manage his own inheritance.

"I assure you, sir, that he is a gentleman."

"Nay, there's nobody who doubted that," Lollio said. "At first sight, I knew him to be a gentleman; he looks no otherwise yet."

The social rank of "gentleman" was desirable.

Lollio may suspect that Antonio was pretending to be a fool. Or he may be saying that gentlemen and fools are interchangeable.

"Let him have good attendance — be looked after well — and sweet lodging," Pedro said.

"As good as my mistress lies in, sir, and as you allow us time and means, we can raise him to the higher degree of discretion," Lollio said.

If Lollio suspected that Antonio was pretending to be a fool so he could stay in Alibius' house, then Lollio may suspect that Antonio was doing that so he could seduce Alibius' wife.

A man who tries to seduce another man's wife tends to be discrete and not let the husband know what he is trying to do.

"There shall no cost be lacking, sir," Pedro said. "All expenses shall be paid."

"He will hardly be stretched up to the wit of a magnifico," Lollio said.

"Hardly" can mean "with difficulty."

"Wit" means "intelligence."

A magnifico is a Venetian magistrate.

"Oh, no, that's not to be expected," Pedro said. "Far shorter will be enough."

"I promise you that I'll make him fit to bear office in five weeks," Lollio said. "I'll undertake to wind him up to the wit of constable."

Constables were proverbially stupid, at least in Elizabethan and Jacobean plays.

"If it should be lower than that, it might serve the turn," Pedro said.

Lollio said:

"No — bah — to make him the equal of a headborough, beadle, or watchman would be only a little better than he is."

A headborough is a petty constable, a beadle is a parish constable, and a watchman is a constable of the watch.

Lollio continued:

"A constable I'll able him: I'll make him fit to be a constable. If he becomes a justice afterwards, let him thank the keeper."

Lollio is the keeper of the fools at Alibius' establishment.

Lollio continued:

"Or I'll go further with you. Say I do bring him up to my own pitch: my own height. Say that I make him as wise as myself."

"Why, there I would have it," Pedro said.

"Well, so be it, either I'll be as arrant — as unmitigated — a fool as he, or he shall be as wise as I, and then I think it will serve his turn — it will be sufficient," Lollio said.

"I do like thy wit surpassingly well," Pedro said.

"Yes, you may," Lollio said. "Yet if I had not been a fool, I would have had more wit than I have, too. Remember what state you find me in."

His state was his profession: a keeper of fools. Lollio was a keeper of fools, and his state was also that of a fool.

"State" also means "status."

"I will, and so I leave you," Pedro said. "Take your best cares of Tony, I beg you."

"Take you no cares — no worries — with you," Alibius said. "Leave all of them with us."

Pedro exited.

"Oh, my cousin's gone; cousin, cousin, oh!" Antonio said.

A cousin can be a 1) a kinsman, or 2) a friend.

"Peace, peace, Tony," Lollio said. "Be quiet. You must not cry, child; you must be whipped if you do. Your cousin is here still; I am your cousin, Tony."

The word "cousin" can mean "friend."

"He, he, then I'll not cry, if thou are my cousin, he, he, he," Antonio said.

"It would be best for me to test his wit a little, so that I may know what form — which school class — to place him in," Lollio said.

"Aye, do, Lollio, do," Alibius said.

Lollio said:

"I must ask him easy questions at first."

He then asked Antonio:

"Tony, how many true — that is, honest — fingers does a tailor have on his right hand?"

"As many as on his left, cousin," Antonio said.

"Good, and how many on both?" Lollio asked.

"Two less than a deuce, cousin," Antonio said.

That is: none.

Lollio said:

"Very well answered."

Tailors had a reputation for being dishonest, and Lollio approved of Antonio's cynical answer.

Lollio then said:

"I come to you again, cousin Tony. How many fools go to a wise man?"

"Go to" can mean 1) make up, or 2) visit.

"Forty in a day sometimes, cousin," Antonio said.

"Forty in a day?" Lollio said. "How do you justify that answer?"

"All who fall out among themselves and go to a lawyer to be made friends," Antonio said.

A proverb stated, "Lawyers' houses are built on the heads of fools."

Lawyers make money from litigation, not from reconciliation; therefore, anyone who goes to a lawyer to settle an argument and be made friends with the person argued with must be a fool.

Lollio said:

"He is a parlous — dangerously clever — fool; he must sit in the fourth form at least, I perceive that."

In the USA, the fourth form would be grade 9, and so students would ordinarily be 14 or 15 years old.

Lollio continued:

"I come again, Tony. How many knaves make an honest man?"

"Make" can mean 1) create, and 2) make up.

"I do not know that, cousin," Antonio said.

Lollio said:

"No, the question is too hard for you. I'll tell you the answer, cousin.

"There's three knaves who may make an honest man, a sergeant, a jailer, and a beadle: The sergeant catches him, the jailer holds him, and the beadle lashes him; and if he is not honest then, the hangman must cure him."

"Ha, ha, ha, that's fine sport, cousin," Antonio said.

"This was too deep a question for the fool, Lollio," Alibius said.

Lollio said:

"Yes, this might have served yourself, although I am the one who says it.

"Once more and you shall go play, Tony."

"Aye, play at push-pin, cousin, ha, he," Antonio said.

"Push-pin is a children's game; it is also slang for sex.

"So thou shall," Lollio said. "Say how many fools are here."

"Two, cousin, thou and I," Antonio said.

Lollio said:

"Nay, you are too forward — too cheeky — there, Tony."

Tony had not included Alibius as a fool, although he had included Lollio.

Lollio then asked:

"Pay close attention to my question: How many fools and knaves are here? A fool before a knave, a fool behind a knave, between every two fools a knave, how many fools, how many knaves?"

"Between every two fools a knave" is ambiguous. It can mean "between every two fools stands a knave" or "between every two fools, one of them is a knave."

If Alibius is not a fool, then he is a knave. Two fools and one knave make three fools and knaves.

Of course, a knave can also be a fool, and vice versa. For example, Lollio and Antonio can be regarded as knaves who are making a fool of Alibius.

"I never learnt so far, cousin," Antonio said.

Alibius said, "Thou are asking him too-hard questions, Lollio."

Lollio said:

"I'll make him understand it easily.

"Cousin, stand there."

"Aye, cousin," Antonio said.

Lollio said to Alibius, "Master, stand next to the fool."

"OK, Lollio," Alibius said, moving into position.

Lollio moved into position and said:

"Here's my place.

"Look closely now, Tony. There is a fool before a knave."

"That's I, cousin," Antonio said, meaning that he was the fool.

Lollio said:

"Here's a fool behind a knave, that's I, and between us two fools there is a knave — that's my master.

"The number is only we three, that's all."

"We three, we three, cousin," Antonio said.

A famous picture of the time was titled *We Three* and showed two fools. The third fool was the viewer.

Madmen shouted from further inside Alibius' house.

"Put his head in the pillory," the first madman shouted. "The bread's too little!"

A pillory is a wooden frame with holes for restraining an offender's head and hands. The pillory was often mounted on a post.

The first madman was complaining about not getting enough food.

"Fly, fly, and he catches the swallow!" the second madman said.

A proverb stated, "Fly and you will catch the sparrow."

Food is swallowed.

"Give her more onion, or the devil put the rope around her crag!" the third madman, a Welshman, said.

The rope can be a hangman's noose or a rope made of onions tied together.

"Her" is stage Welsh for "me" and "my." The third madman wanted more food — or a rope that he could use to hang himself.

A crag is a neck.

All three madmen were concerned with food.

Lollio said, "You may hear what time of day it is: The chimes of Bedlam sound."

Bedlam is St. Mary of Bethlehem Hospital; it was a lunatic asylum.

The "chimes of Bedlam" are the cries of the madmen.

"Peace, peace, or the wire — the whip made out of wire — comes!" Alibius said to the madmen.

The third madman, a Welshman, said, "Cat whore, cat whore, her parmasant, her parmasant!"

A mouse had eaten his parmesan cheese, and he was insulting the cat for letting it happen.

A "cather" ["cat whore"] is dialect for a scaffolding. Gallows have scaffolds. The word comes from the Welsh *cader*, which can mean "wooden frame."

"Cat whore" is also close in pronunciation to "captor."

A stereotype of the Welsh is that they *really* liked cheese.

Alibius said:

"Peace, I say! Silence!

"Their hour's come; they must be fed, Lollio."

Lollio said, "There's no hope of recovery of that Welsh madman: He was undone and ruined by a mouse that spoiled him a parmasant; he has lost his wits because of it."

"Go to your charge, Lollio," Alibius said. "I'll go to mine."

Lollio said, "You go to your madmen's ward; let me alone with your fools. Leave them to me."

"And remember my last charge, Lollio," Alibius said.

His last charge — order — to Lollio was to spy on Alibius' wife and make sure that she did not cuckold him.

Alibius exited.

Lollio said:

"Of which of your patients do you think I am?"

In other words: Did Alibius think that he — Lollio — was a fool, or a madman?

Lollio said:

"Come, Tony, you must go among your school-fellows now. There's pretty scholars among them, I can tell you. There's some of them at *stultus, stulta, stultum.*"

"Pretty" can mean "clever."

Stultus, stulta, stultum was the Latin declension for the adjective "foolish." It is only the second declension (of five), so the madmen have much more Latin to learn.

"I would like to see the madmen, cousin, if they would not bite me," Antonio said.

"No, they shall not bite thee, Tony," Lollio said.

"They bite when they are at dinner, don't they, coz?" Antonio asked.

"Coz" means "cousin."

"They bite at dinner indeed, Tony," Lollio said. "Well, I hope to get credit by thee; I like thee the best of all the scholars whom I ever brought up, and thou shall prove to be a wise man, or I'll prove to be a fool myself."

They exited.

CHAPTER 2

— 2.1 —

Beatrice and Jasperino met each other in a room in the castle.

Beatrice said, "Oh, sir, I'm ready now for that fair service that makes the name of friend sit glorious on you. May good angels and this conduct be your guide. Fitness of time and place is there set down, sir."

Beatrice wanted to arrange a meeting with Alsemero.

She handed Jasperino a paper. The paper was Alsemero's conduct: It was a paper that contained directions and the time when Alsemero could see her in her private chamber. The conduct was also a pass authorizing Alsemero to see her there: He would meet Diaphanta, Beatrice's serving-woman, at a certain time and place, and she would escort him there.

"The joy I shall return rewards my service," Jasperino said.

His delivering the conduct to Alsemero would make both Beatrice and Alsemero happy.

When Beatrice had mentioned "good angels," she may have offered him some gold coins that were called angels.

Jasperino wanted nothing for himself.

He exited.

Alone, Beatrice said to herself:

"How wise is Alsemero in his friend! It is a sign he makes his choice of a friend with judgment. Then I appear in nothing more justified than in making my choice of him. For it is a principle that he who can choose that bosom friend well, who partakes of his thoughts, proves to be most discreet in every choice he makes."

In this society, the word "friend" can mean "lover." Beatrice wanted to be Alsemero's "friend."

Beatrice continued:

"I think that I love now with the eyes of judgment and see the way to recognize merit — I clearly see it. A true deserver sparkles like a luminous diamond: In darkness you may see him who is in absence, which is the greatest darkness that falls on love. Yet he is best discerned then with intellectual eyesight."

"Intellectual eyesight" is what the mind sees or imagines.

Beatrice continued saying to herself:

"Who is Piracquo, whom my father expends and wastes his breath extolling? And my father's blessing is only mine as I regard his name, else his blessing goes away from me, and turns head as an enemy against me, transformed into a curse."

Beatrice was saying that she would get her father's blessing only by marrying well; that is, she would get her father's blessing only if she married Alonzo de Piracquo.

Beatrice continued:

"Some speedy way must be remembered; I must think of a way to get out of this upcoming marriage.

"He's — my father is — so forward, too, so urgent and eager and importunate that way, that he scarcely allows me breath to speak to my new comforts."

Alonso was also "forward" — he was eager to quickly marry Beatrice.

Her new comforts — delights and pleasures — are those that would come from and with Alsemero.

Deflores entered the scene.

He said to himself:

"Yonder she is. Whatever ails me? Now recently especially I can as well be hanged as refrain from seeing her. Some twenty times a day, nay, not so little, do I invent errands to force myself into her presence, frame ways and excuses to come into her sight, and I have small reason for doing it, and less encouragement from her, for she baits and taunts me always every time worse than the previous time. She does profess herself to be the cruelest enemy to my face in town. At no hand — on no account, and neither close at hand nor far away — can she abide the sight of me, as if danger, or ill luck, hung in my looks.

"I must confess my face is bad enough, but I know far worse faces that have had better fortune, and are not just endured, but are doted on. And yet such pick-haired faces, with chins like witches', with here and there five hairs whispering in a corner, as if they grew in fear one of another, wrinkles like troughs, where swine deformity [pig-like ugliness] swills the tears of perjury that lie there like wash [watery discharge, or liquid food for pigs], fallen from the slimy and dishonest eye. Yet such a one plucks sweets — enjoys women — without restraint and has the grace of beauty to his sweet."

As an adjective, the word "pick" means "choice" or "best," but this beard is sparse: "with here and there five hairs whispering in a corner."

Possibly, this beard is a "pict-beard": a chin that looks as if a few hairs have been painted on it.

Possibly, the "beard" is made mostly of spots that look as if they are painted on. Deflores has a skin condition, and his "beard" may be made of acne and a few hairs.

Or perhaps it is a "picked-beard": a beard from which most of the hairs have been picked. Think of much-tweezed eyebrows.

"Has the grace of beauty to his sweet" may mean 1) His sweetheart thinks that he is handsome, 2) His sweetheart is beautiful.

"Grace" can also mean "prayer," as in blessing a meal, and "sweet" can mean a sweet dessert.

Deflores continued saying to himself:

"Though my hard fate has thrust me out to servitude, I tumbled into the world a gentleman."

He was born with the rank of gentleman, but he served Beatrice's father.

In this society, gentlemen without financial means often served as high-ranking servants to other, wealthy gentlemen.

Beatrice noticed his presence, and Deflores said to himself:

"She turns her blessed eye upon me now, and I'll endure all storms before I part with it."

Beatrice said out loud:

"Again!"

She then said to herself:

"This ominous ill-faced fellow disturbs me more than all my other passions!"

"Passions" can mean 1) sufferings, 2) strong emotions, and/or 3) sexual passions.

"Now it begins again," Deflores said. "I'll stand this storm of hail although the stones pelt me."

"Thy business? What's thy business?" Beatrice asked Deflores.

Deflores said to himself:

"Soft and fair."

In other words: Speak softly and calmly, and speak good words to her.

Proverbs 15:1 states, *A soft answer turneth away wrath: but grievous words stir up anger*" (King James Version).

Deflores continued saying to himself:

"I cannot part so soon now."

Beatrice said to herself:

"The villain's transfixed."

She said out loud:

"Thou standing toad-pool!"

A standing toad-pool was a pool of stagnant water, from which this society believed that toads were engendered.

Deflores said to himself, "The shower of insults falls with full force now."

Angry, Beatrice said, "Who sent thee? What's thy errand? Leave my sight!"

"My lord your father ordered me to deliver a message to you," Deflores said.

Beatrice said:

"What! Another, since the last one? Yet again?"

Previously, Deflores had delivered the message that her father was coming to her. Her father had come and had met Alsemero.

Beatrice ordered:

"Do it and be hanged then — let me be rid of thee!"

"True service merits mercy," Deflores said.

A true lover hopes for [sexual] mercy from the woman he loves. So says Deflores.

"What's thy message?" Beatrice asked.

"Let beauty settle but in patience — be patient, beautiful one, please," Deflores said. "You shall hear all."

"A dallying, trifling torment!" Beatrice said.

"Dallying" can mean 1) chattering, or 2) flirting.

Beatrice's torment was listening to Deflores.

Deflores began the message: "Signior Alonzo de Piracquo, lady, sole brother to Tomazo de Piracquo —"

Beatrice interrupted, "— slave, when will thou make an end?"

"Too soon I shall," Deflores said.

He would deliver his message too quickly for him: After he delivered the message, he would have to leave her presence.

Also, like so many others, he would die all too soon.

"What all this while of him?" Beatrice asked.

Deflores began, "The said Alonzo, with the foresaid Tomazo —"

"Yet again!" Beatrice said.

Deflores was repeating what he had already said.

Deflores finished, "— has newly alighted from his horse."

Alonzo and Tomazo had come to visit Beatrice and her father.

"May vengeance strike the news!" Beatrice said. "Thou thing most loathed, what reason was there in this to bring thee within my sight?"

"My lord your father ordered me to seek you out," Deflores said.

"Was there no other person to send his errand by?" complained Beatrice.

"It seems it is my luck to always be in the way," Deflores said.

"Get thee away from me," Beatrice said.

Deflores said:

"So be it."

He then said to himself:

"Why, aren't I an ass to devise ways thus to be railed at and insulted? I must see her always. I shall have a mad qualm within this hour again, I know it, and like a common Garden bull, I do but take breath to be lugged — pulled — by the hair or ears again."

His "mad qualm" was likely a pang of lust.

Bulls (and bears) were baited — tormented — by dogs at the Paris Garden. This "sport" was called bull-baiting (or bear-baiting).

Deflores continued saying to himself:

"What this may bode and foretell I don't know; I'll despair the less because there are daily precedents of bad faces that are beloved beyond all reason.

"These foul chops — ugly mouth and cheeks — of mine may come into favor one day among his fellows. Wrangling — bitter arguing — has proved to be the mistress of good pastime. As children cry themselves asleep, I have seen women who have chid — scolded — themselves to bed to men."

Make-up sex after an argument can be passionate.

Deflores exited.

Alone, Beatrice said to herself:

"I never see this fellow but I think of some harm coming towards me. Danger's in my mind still; I scarcely stop trembling for an hour afterward. The next good mood I find my father in, I'll get Deflores quite discarded.

"Oh, I was lost in this small disturbance and forgot affliction's fiercer torrent that now comes to bear down all my comforts!"

"Affliction's fiercer torrent" was Alonzo, Beatrice's betrothed, whom she no longer loved.

Vermandero, Alonzo, and Tomazo entered the scene.

Alonzo and Tomazo were brothers.

Vermandero said to Alonzo and Tomazo:

"You are both welcome."

He then said to Alonzo:

"But a special welcome belongs to you, sir, to whose most noble name our love presents the additional title of 'son': our son Alonzo."

Alonzo and Beatrice were betrothed, and so Alonzo was expected to become Vermandero's son-in-law.

"The treasury of honorific titles cannot bring forth a title I should more rejoice in, sir," Alonzo said.

Vermandero said:

"You have improved — enhanced — it well.

"Daughter, prepare yourself. The day will steal upon thee suddenly."

Beatrice said to herself, "However, I will be sure to keep the night, if it should come so near me."

"Keep the night" is ambiguous.

According to the *Oxford English Dictionary*, "Keep" means both of these things:

1) "To meet in resistance or opposition; to encounter."

2) "To intercept or meet in a friendly way; to greet, welcome."

Since Beatrice did not love Alonzo, "keep the night" probably meant that their wedding night would be a hostile encounter. But since Beatrice can be passionate, sex on her wedding night could be something she would welcome.

Vermandero and Beatrice talked apart from the others.

Tomazo said, "Alonzo."

"Brother," Alonzo replied.

Tomazo said, "Truly, I see small welcome in her eye."

Alonzo said:

"Bah, you are too severe a censurer and critic of love in all points and respects. There's no persuading you that if lovers should find fault with everything, affection would be like an ill-set book, whose faults might prove as big as half the volume."

An "ill-set" book is badly typeset. The faults are a list of misprints.

Beatrice said, "That's all I entreat and ask for."

Vermandero replied:

"It is only reasonable. I'll see what my son says about it."

He then said to Alonzo, his prospective son-in-law:

"Son Alonzo, here's a proposal made just to reprieve a maidenhead for three days longer."

In other words: Beatrice wanted the marriage to be held not right away, but in three days.

Vermandero continued:

"The request is not far out of reason, for indeed the former time is pinching and pressing."

Alonzo said, "Although my joys will be set back so much time as I could wish they had been set forward, yet since she desires it, the time is set as pleasing as before. I find no gladness lacking."

Vermandero said:

"May I ever meet it in that point still."

In other words: "May I always and forever make you glad in such matters."

He then said to Tomazo and Alonzo:

"You are nobly welcome, sirs."

Vermandero and Beatrice exited.

"So, did you notice the dullness of her parting now?" Tomazo asked.

Tomazo detected in Beatrice a lack of interest concerning Alonzo.

"What dullness?" Alonzo asked. "Thou are always so quick to make objections."

"Why, let it go then," Tomazo said. "I am just a fool to notice your harms so heedfully."

"Where's my oversight?" Alonzo asked. "What am I not seeing?"

Tomazo said:

"Come, your faith's deceived in her, strongly deceived. Detach your affection with all speed that wisdom can bring to it; your peace is ruined otherwise.

"Think what a torment it is to marry one whose heart has leapt into another's bosom. If ever she receives sexual pleasure from thee, it comes not in thy name, nor of thy gift. She lies only with another in thine arms. He is the half-father to all thy children in the conception; if he does not beget children, she helps to get them [children] for him [the man she really loves] in his [Alonzo's, her husband's sexual] passions, and how dangerous and shameful her restraint may go in time to, it is not to be thought on without sufferings."

Whenever Beatrice would have sex with Alonzo, she would be thinking not about him, but about the man she loved.

During the conception of children, she would be conceiving in her mind the image of the man she loved (not Alonso), and so in a way that man would be the half-father of the children.

And if she — or Alonzo — tried to restrain her feelings for the other man, her passions would break out in dangerous and shameful ways that would cause pain.

"You speak as if she loved some other man, then," Alonzo said.

"Do you apprehend — understand — so slowly?" Tomazo asked.

Alonzo said:

"Nay, if that is your only fear, I am safe enough.

"Preserve your friendship and your counsel, brother, for times of more distress.

"I would depart as a dangerous, deadly enemy to any but thyself who should just *think* that my betrothed knew the meaning of inconstancy, much less the use and practice of inconstancy. Yet we are friends."

"Use" can refer to the sex act.

Alonzo continued:

"Please let no more be urged. I can endure much until I meet an insult to her, and then I am not myself.

"Farewell, sweet brother. How much we are bound and obligated to Heaven for our departing lovingly as friends and brothers!"

Alonzo exited.

Tomazo said, "Why, here is love's tame madness! Thus a man quickly steals into his vexation and trouble."

Tomazo exited.

— 2.2 —

In another room in the palace, Diaphanta and Alsemero met together.

Diaphanta said:

"The place is my responsibility. You have kept your hour; may the reward of a just — a right and proper — meeting bless you.

"I hear my lady coming.

"Complete and perfect gentleman, I dare not be too busy with my praises of you. There are dangerous things to deal with."

Her praises of Alsemero could be dangerous because Beatrice could overhear them and be jealous.

"Things" can be sex organs, and "deal with" can mean "have sex with."

Diaphanta exited.

"This goes well," Alsemero said. "These women are the ladies' cabinets. Things of most precious trust are locked in them."

"Cabinets" are "secret receptacles." Here, metaphorically, they are confidantes.

Beatrice entered the scene.

She said to Alsemero:

"I have within my eyesight all my desires.

"Requests that holy prayers ascend Heaven for, and brings them down to furnish our defects, come not more sweet to our necessities than thou unto my wishes."

Beatrice's way of expressing herself can be convoluted.

In less-convoluted words: Holy prayers ascend to Heaven with requests, and after the holy prayers are granted, they come down to Earth to furnish us with what we lack. Those granted requests do not come sweeter to our necessities than thou who come to grant my wishes.

"We are so alike in our expressions, lady, that unless I borrow the same words, I shall never find their equals," Alsemero said.

Beatrice said:

"How happy would be this meeting, this embrace, if it were free from enmity and hatred!"

She kissed him and then said:

"This poor kiss — it has an enemy, a hateful one who wishes poison to it."

That enemy is Alonzo de Piracquo, who of course does not want his betrothed to have an affair with another man.

Beatrice continued:

"How well would I be now if there were no such name known as Piracquo, nor no such tie as the command of parents! I should be but too much blessed."

Alsemero said, "One good service would strike off both your fears, and I'll go near it and say what it is, too, since you are so distressed. Remove the cause, and the command ceases, so there's two fears blown out with one and the same blast."

Fetters can be struck off, and debts can be struck off a list.

An axiom of Scholastic philosophers was "remove the cause and the effect ceases."

One blast of breath can blow out two candles, and one killing can remove two obstacles.

If Alonzo were to die, Beatrice's father could not make her marry him, and so Beatrice would be able to be happy. Two fears would be blown out.

One of Beatrice's fears concerned Alonzo; the other fear concerned her father.

"Please let me know what you mean, sir," Beatrice said. "What might that so strangely happy service be?"

The service would be "happy" because it would have what Beatrice considered good consequences.

Alsemero said, "The most honorable part of a man: valor. I'll send a challenge to Piracquo immediately."

This was a challenge to duel.

Beatrice said, "What! Do you call that the extinguishing of fear when it is the only way to keep it flaming? Aren't you at risk in the action — you who are all my joys and comforts?

"Please say no more, sir. Say you prevailed, the danger is yours and not mine then. The law against dueling would claim you from me, or obscurity as an exile or a fugitive from the law would be made the grave to bury you alive.

"I'm glad these thoughts come forth; oh, don't keep even one thought of this dangerous kind, sir! Don't even think about dueling!

"Here was a course of action found to bring sorrow on her way to death."

This course of action would bring sorrow and death. Beatrice would die of grief.

Beatrice continued out loud:

"The tears would never have dried until the dust of the grave had choked them. Blood-guiltiness is appropriate to a fouler visage, and now I think about one —"

Beatrice said to herself:

"— I was too blameworthy. I have marred so good a market with my scorn. It would have been done without question. Creation framed even the ugliest creature for some use, yet to see I could not mark so much where it should be."

Beatrice was thinking that she could have used Deflores — who had a "fouler visage" or uglier face — to murder Alonzo. But she had marred that market — lost that opportunity — because she had not had the idea of manipulating him until just now. She had not seen and realized to what use Deflores could be put.

"Lady," Alsemero said.

Beatrice continued speaking to herself, "Why, men of art make much of poison. Keep one to expel another. Where was my art?"

This society believed that one poison could be used to counteract another poison.

A proverb stated, "One poison expels [drives out] another."

The word "art" can mean 1) science, and 2) cunning.

Beatrice was criticizing herself for not realizing earlier that she could have manipulated Deflores to do evil deeds for her.

"Lady, you do not hear me," Alsemero said. "You aren't listening to me."

Beatrice said:

"I do especially hear you, sir."

Indeed, she was giving much thought to Alsemero's suggestion that Alonzo might be removed by being killed.

Beatrice continued:

"The present times are not so securely on our side as those may be hereafter; we must use them then as thrifty folks use their wealth, sparingly now until our time comes and becomes more favorable."

"You teach wisdom, lady," Alsemero said.

Beatrice called, "Within there, Diaphanta!"

Diaphanta entered the scene.

"Do you call me, madam?" she asked.

Beatrice said, "Perfect your service, and conduct this gentleman the private way you brought him."

"Perfect your service" means "complete your duties."

Diaphanta had brought Alsemero a private way to visit Beatrice; now she would take him back that same way.

The word "service" can mean "sex."

The phrase "private way" also suggests a sexual liaison.

"I shall, madam," Diaphanta said.

"My love's as firm as love ever built upon," Alsemero said.

Erections are firm.

Diaphanta and Alsemero exited.

Deflores entered the scene. He had been eavesdropping.

He said to himself:

"I have watched this meeting, and I wonder much what shall become of the other: Alonzo. I'm sure both cannot be sexually served unless Beatrice transgresses and sleeps with both men.

"Happily then I'll put in for one of her lovers, for if a woman should fly from one point, then away from him she makes a 'husband.'"

One meaning of "point" is a "penis." It can also mean "decimal point."

According to the *Oxford English Dictionary*, in falconry, "point" means "Of a hawk, the action of rising vertically in the air to mark the position of the quarry."

Continuing to use some words from falconry, Deflores continued speaking to himself:

"She spreads and mounts then like arithmetic — one, ten, one hundred, one thousand, ten thousand — and she proves in time sutler to an army royal."

"Spread" can mean 1) multiply, and 2) beget.

The decimal point moves as the woman adds lovers: 1.0 to 10.0 to 100.0 to 1000.0 to 10,000.0.

Beatrice can spread her legs and she can sexually mount a man — make that many men. Eventually she will figuratively prove to be a sutler — a seller of supplies, or a whore — to an army royal — a very large army of men.

Deflores continued speaking to himself:

"Now I expect to be most richly railed at and insulted, yet I must see her."

Beatrice said to herself:

"Why, put the case — suppose — I loathed him as much as youth and beauty hates a sepulcher. Must I necessarily show it? Can't I keep that secret, and serve my turn upon him?"

The word "case" can mean "vagina."

The word "secret" can mean "private part."

The phrase "serve my turn" can mean 1) "use for my own purposes," or 2) "have sex with."

Beatrice then said to herself:

"See, he's here."

She said out loud:

"Deflores."

Deflores said to himself, "Ha, I shall run mad with joy! She called me fairly by my name, Deflores, and she called me neither rogue nor rascal."

Beatrice complimented him: "What have you done to your face recently? You have met with some good physician. You have pruned — that is, preened — yourself, I think. In the past, you have not looked so amorously."

Beatrice was using the respectful "you" to refer to Deflores instead of using "thou."

"Looked so amorously" can mean "looked so desirable."

Deflores said to himself:

"Not I. I have not been treated by a physician.

"This is the same physiognomy and face to a hair and pimple that she called scurvy scarcely an hour ago."

"What is this? What's going on?"

"Come here," Beatrice said. "Nearer, man."

"I'm up to the chin in Heaven!" Deflores said to himself.

His private parts were not in Heaven.

"Turn, let me see you," Beatrice said. "Fah! It is just the heat — the inflammation — of the liver, I perceive it. I thought it had been worse."

This society regarded the liver as the seat of violent passions.

The worse disease she thought of may be venereal disease.

"Her fingers touched me," Deflores said to himself. "She smells all of ambergris."

Ambergris is used in the making of perfume.

"I'll make a medicinal lotion, for you shall cleanse this — your skin — within a fortnight," Beatrice said.

"You will make it with your own hands, lady?" Deflores asked.

"Yes, with my own hands, sir," Beatrice said. "In a work of cure, I'll trust no other."

Deflores said to himself, "It is half an act of pleasure to hear her talk thus to me."

Sex is an act of pleasure.

Beatrice said, "When we are used to a hard — an ugly — face, it is not so unpleasing. It mends still in opinion, hourly mends. I see it by experience."

Deflores said to himself, "I was blest to light upon this minute; I'll make use of it."

To "make use" of something can mean to "have sex" with it.

"Hardness — ugliness — becomes the visage of a man well," Beatrice said. "It argues service, resolution, manhood, if the cause of the hardness were of employment."

"Employment" can mean "sex."

Hardness is used in sex.

Deflores said, "It would be soon seen, if ever your ladyship had cause to use it. I would but wish the honor of a service so happy as that mounts to."

Hmm.

Deflores' hardness would be soon seen, if ever Beatrice had cause to have sex with it. And yes, Deflores would get "on her" (honor), and sexual mounting would be involved.

Beatrice said to herself:

"We shall try you."

She meant that she would test him to see if she could manipulate him, but "try" can also mean "try out in bed."

Beatrice said out loud:

"Oh, my Deflores!"

Deflores said to himself:

"What's that? She calls me hers already: 'my Deflores'!"

He said out loud:

"You were about to sigh out something, madam."

"No, was I?" Beatrice said. "I forgot. Oh!"

"There it is again, the very fellow of your previous sigh!" Deflores said.

"You are too quick — too apprehensive — sir," Beatrice said.

"There's no excuse — no evasion — for it, now that I have heard it twice, madam," Deflores said. "That sigh would eagerly have utterance. Take pity on your sigh and lend it a free word — speak for it. Alas, how it labors for liberty! I hear the murmur yet beat at your bosom."

Deflores was interpreting Beatrice's sighs as indications of her sexual desire for him.

Beatrice began, "I wish creation —"

"Aye, well said, that's it," Deflores said.

He was thinking of procreation.

Beatrice continued, "— had made me a man and not a woman."

"Nay, that's not it," Deflores said.

Deflores wanted Beatrice to be a woman.

"Oh, being a man is the soul of freedom!" Beatrice said. "I would not then be forced to marry a man I hate beyond all depths. I would have the power then to oppose my loathings, indeed, to remove them forever from my sight."

Deflores said:

"Oh, blest occasion and opportunity!"

He knelt before Beatrice and said:

"Without change to your sex, you have your wishes. Claim so much man in me."

He was willing to do what she said she would do if she were a man.

"In thee, Deflores?" Beatrice said. "There's small cause for that."

"Don't put it away from me," Deflores said. "It's a service that I kneel for to you."

"You are too violent and passionate to intend faithful service to me," Beatrice said. "There's horror in my service; there's blood and danger. Can those be things to sue for?"

"If you knew how sweet it would be to me to be employed in any act of yours, you would say then I failed and was not reverent enough when I received your request to do it," Deflores said.

The word "act" can mean "act of sex."

Beatrice said to herself:

"This is much, I think."

She was surprised by the intensity of Deflores' desire to serve her, and she now attributed it to desire and need for money:

"Perhaps his wants are greedy, and to such men as that gold tastes like angels' food."

Angels' food is manna: bread from Heaven.

Psalm 78:24-25 (King James Version) states:

24 And had rained down manna upon them to eat, and had given them of the corn of heaven.

25 Man did eat angels' food: he sent them meat [food] to the full.

Beatrice said to Deflores:

"Rise."

Still kneeling, Deflores said, "I'll have the work first."

Beatrice had said enough that he knew the work would be illegal and dangerous. He could guess that she meant murder.

Beatrice said to herself:

"Possibly his need for money is strong upon him."

She gave him money and said:

"There's something to encourage thee.

"To the degree that thou are courageous and thy service is dangerous, thy reward shall be precious."

Beatrice meant a financial reward.

Deflores said, "I have thought about my reward; I have assured myself of that beforehand, and I know it will be precious. The thought ravishes!"

Deflores meant a sexual reward: a ravishing reward.

"Then take him to thy fury," Beatrice said.

"I thirst for him," Deflores said.

"Alonzo de Piracquo," Beatrice said.

"His end is upon him," Deflores said as he rose. "He shall be seen no more."

"How lovely — beautiful and lovable — thou now appear to me!" Beatrice said. "Never was a man more dearly rewarded than you will be."

The word "dearly" can also mean 1) "grievously," and 2) "painfully."

"I do think about that," Deflores said.

"Be wondrously careful in the execution," Beatrice said.

"Why, are not both our lives upon the cast?" Deflores asked.

He meant a metaphorical cast of a die.

He would be careful because his life and Beatrice's life would end if he failed.

"Then I throw all my fears upon thy service," Beatrice said.

"They never shall rise to hurt you," Deflores said.

"When the deed's done, I'll furnish thee with all things for thy flight," Beatrice said. "Thou may live splendidly in another country."

By "deed," Beatrice meant "murder."

"Aye, aye, we'll talk about that hereafter," Deflores said.

By "that," he meant "deed," by which he meant sex.

Beatrice said to herself: "I shall rid myself of two inveterate loathings at one time: Piracquo and his — Deflores' — dog-face."

She exited.

Deflores said:

"Oh, my blood!"

His "blood" was sexual passion.

Deflores continued saying to himself:

"I think I feel her in my arms already, her wanton fingers combing out this beard, and being pleased, praising this bad face!"

Possibly, "this beard" was his pubic hair. That may be the case if his facial beard consisted of many pimples and a few hairs.

Deflores continued:

"Because of the power of hunger and [sexual] pleasure, they'll commend sometimes slovenly prepared and lewd dishes and feed heartily on them. Nay, which is stranger, they will refuse daintier dishes [including men] for them. Some women are odd feeders.

"I'm too loud. Here comes the man who goes supperless to bed, yet he shall not rise tomorrow to his dinner."

Deflores planned to kill Alonzo before supper.

Alonzo entered the scene.

"Deflores," Alonzo said.

"My kind, honorable lord," Deflores said.

"I am glad I have met with thee," Alonzo said.

"Sir," Deflores said.

"Can thou show me the full strength of the castle?" Alonzo asked.

"That I can, sir," Deflores said.

"I much desire it," Alonzo said.

Deflores said, "And if the ways and straits of some of the passages are not too tedious — that is, troublesome — for you, I will assure you it will be worth your time and sight, my lord."

"Ways" are pathways between walls, and "straits" are narrow parts in the pathways.

"Bah, that shall be no hindrance," Alonso said.

"I'm your servant then," Deflores said. "It is now almost dinner time; in preparation for when your lordship rises from the table, I'll have the keys on me."

"Thanks, kind Deflores," Alonzo said.

Deflores said to himself, "He's safely thrust upon me beyond my hopes."

Deflores would be able to kill Alonzo in the ways and straits: in a place where there would be no witnesses. He could not have hoped for a better opportunity.

They exited.

Deflores returned and hid a naked — unsheathed — rapier.

CHAPTER 3

— 3.1 —

Alonzo and Deflores stood in a narrow passage.

Deflores said:

"Yes, here are all the keys. I was afraid, my lord, that I didn't have the key for the postern — this is that key."

A postern is a side or back entrance.

Deflores continued:

"I've all, I have all the keys, my lord. This key is for the sconce."

According to the *Oxford English Dictionary*, a sconce is "A small fort or earthwork; esp. one built to defend a ford, pass, castle-gate, etc., or erected as a counter-fort."

"This is a very spacious and impregnable fort," Alonzo said.

Deflores said:

"You'll tell me more praise when you've seen more of it, my lord.

"This descent is somewhat narrow. We shall never pass well with our weapons; they'll only trouble us."

Deflores took off his sword.

"Thou say the truth," Alonzo said.

"Please let me help your lordship take off your sword," Deflores said.

He helped take off Alonzo's sword and sword-belt.

"It's done," Alonzo said. "Thanks, kind Deflores."

"Here are hooks, my lord, whose purpose is to hang such things," Deflores said.

He hung up the swords.

"Lead," Alonzo said. "I'll follow thee."

Deflores led the way.

Deflores and Alonzo stood in a vault with a casement.

According to the *Oxford English Dictionary*, a casemate [another spelling of "casement"] is "A fortified chamber, often built within a fortress wall or projecting from it, provided with embrasures for defence; such a chamber used as a magazine, barracks, prison, etc."

Also according to *Oxford English Dictionary*, a casemate is "An opening through which missiles may be discharged; an embrasure."

A casement is a window or something likened to a window.

The casement Deflores and Alonzo were in was a fortified chamber with an opening through which one could look out.

Deflores said, "All this is nothing; you shall see soon a place you little dream about."

That place is the grave.

"I am glad I have this leisure," Alonzo said. "All in your master's house imagine I have taken a gondola."

A gondola is a small boat.

Deflores said:

"All but myself, sir."

He said to himself:

"Which makes me safe and secure."

He then said out loud to Alonzo:

"My lord, I'll place you at a casement here, which will show you the full strength of all the castle."

"Look, and spend your time looking a while upon that object."

"Here's rich variety, Deflores," Alonzo said.

"Yes, sir," Deflores said.

"This is goodly munition," Alonzo said. "This is a splendid fortification."

According to the *Oxford English Dictionary*, "munition" means "Military equipment of any kind, as weaponry, ammunition, stores, etc. Now usually in *plural*."

"Aye, there's ordnance, sir. No bastard — impure — metal will ring for you a peal like bells at great men's funerals."

According to the *Oxford English Dictionary*, "ordnance" means "Military materials, stores, or supplies; implements of war; missiles discharged in war (also in *plural*)."

Alonzo was looking through a window at some fortifications of the castle, including a sconce that had been built to protect the castle gate. Much cannon was visible.

The view from the casement did not show "the full strength of all the castle," although it did show much or all of the strength of the sconce protecting the castle gate. Of course, it did not show Deflores' hidden rapier.

The "peal" is a discharge of cannon, which Deflores compared to the peal of bells. To Deflores, the sound of these cannon firing was as beautiful as the peal of bells.

Deflores continued:

"Keep your eye straight ahead, my lord. Take special notice of that sconce before you. There you may dwell awhile."

"Dwell" can mean 1) dwell in thought, and 2) dwell after death.

"I am upon it," Alonzo said.

He meant that he was looking upon the sconce.

"And so am I," Deflores said.

He meant that he was ready to set upon the work of killing Alonzo.

He got the sword he had hidden, and he stabbed Alonzo.

"Deflores, oh, Deflores, whose malice and hatred have thou put on?" Alonzo asked. "Who had you do this?"

"Do you question a work of secrecy?" Deflores said. "I must silence you."

He stabbed Alonzo again.

Alonzo cried out, "Oh! Oh! Oh!"

Deflores said:

"I must silence you."

He stabbed Alonzo a third time, and Alonzo died.

Deflores then said:

"So, here's an undertaking well accomplished. This vault serves to good use now. Ha! What's that which threw sparkles in my eye? Oh, it is a diamond he wears upon his finger. It was well found. This will prove I did the work."

Deflores tried to take the diamond ring off Alonzo's finger.

Deflores said:

"What, so fast on? It will not part from Alonzo in death?"

Earlier, Beatrice had said, "A true deserver sparkles like a luminous diamond: In darkness you may see him who is in absence, which is the greatest darkness that falls on love."

Also, of course, marriages are supposed to last "until death do us part."

Deflores continued:

"I'll take a speedy course then: Finger and all shall come off."

He cut off Alonzo's finger and diamond ring.

Deflores said:

"So, now I'll clear the passages from all suspicion or fear."

He carried away Alonzo's body.

Isabella and Lollio talked together in a room in Alibius' house. Isabella was Alibius' young wife.

Lollio being Lollio, expect bawdiness.

Isabella said, "Why, sirrah? From where do you have the commission to fetter — to lock — the doors against me? If you keep me in a cage, please whistle to me as if I were a caged bird. Let me be doing something."

"Sirrah" was a title used to address someone of a social rank inferior to the speaker. Friends, however, could use it to refer to each other.

Lollio was not allowing her to leave the house.

The word "doing " can refer to sex.

"Something" can be "some thing."

A "thing" is a sex organ; it can be male or female.

Lollio said:

"You shall be doing, if it pleases you."

By "pleases," Lollio meant "sexually pleases."

Lollio continued:

"I'll whistle to you if you'll pipe after me."

"Pipe after me" means "whistle after I have finished," or "sing to me," or "play after me" or "follow my lead."

A common phrase of the time stated, "To dance after a person's pipe."

"Dance" can mean "have sex," and "pipe" can mean "penis."

Isabella could "pipe" on Lollio's pipe by putting it in her mouth.

"Is it your master's pleasure, or your own, to keep me in this pinfold?" Isabella said.

A "pinfold" is a fenced enclosure for stray cattle, but a "pin" can be a penis.

"It is for my master's pleasure, lest being taken in another man's corn, you might be pounded in another place," Lollio said.

A stray cow that got into a corn field belonging to another man (not the owner) could be impounded in a pinfold.

Lollio, of course, was talking about sexual pounding.

"It is very well, and he'll prove to be very wise," Isabella said.

"He says that if you please to be sociable, you have company enough, in the house, of all sorts of people," Lollio said.

"Of all sorts?" Isabella said. "Why, here's no one but fools and madmen."

"Very well," Lollio said, "and where will you find any other, if you should go abroad — out of the house? There's my master, and there's I, too."

"You two are one of each kind: a madman and a fool," Isabella said.

Lollio said, "I would even participate as both madman and fool then if I were as you. I know you are half-mad already; be half-foolish, too."

"Participate" means "share the nature of."

When two people marry, they become one. One half of Isabella-Alibius was mad.

But "participate" can also mean "share," and Lollio would like Isabella to share herself sexually with both her husband (the madman) and Lollio (the fool).

Isabella said:

"You are a brave, saucy — bold and impertinent — rascal!

"Come on, sir, afford me — give me — then the pleasure of your bedlam. You were commending once today to me your most recently arrived lunatic: what a proper and handsome body there was without brains to guide it, and what a pitiful delight appears in your description of that defect, as if your wisdom had found a mirth in madness."

She did not like Lollio's mocking of madmen.

Isabella continued:

"Please, sir, let me partake if there is such a pleasure."

Lollio replied, "If I do not show you the handsomest, most discreet madman, one whom I may call the understanding madman, then say I am a fool."

Isabella said, "Well, it's a match — it's a deal. I will say so."

She will say that Lollio is a fool.

Lollio said, "When you have a taste of the madman, you shall, if you please, see Fools' College on the other side. I seldom lock there; it is but shooting a bolt or two, and you are among them."

On one side of the asylum were the madmen, and on the other side were the fools.

Lollio did not often lock them up, and there were only one or two bolts to draw back to unlock them.

"Shooting a bolt" also means "shooting an arrow," which has a bawdy meaning of ejaculation.

A proverb stated, "A fool's bolt [arrow] is soon shot."

Lollio exited.

Inside, he said to the handsome madman, "Come on, sir, let me see how handsomely you'll behave yourself now."

Lollio returned with Franciscus, the handsome madman.

Franciscus looked at Isabella and said:

"How sweetly she looks! Oh, but there's a wrinkle in her brow as deep as philosophy."

The wrinkle is unlikely to be deep, and so Franciscus — the madman — does not believe that philosophy is metaphorically deep.

He then looked at Lollio and said:

"Anacreon, drink to my mistress' health; I'll pledge it. Wait, wait, there's a poisonous spider in the cup! No, it is only a grape-stone. Swallow it, and fear nothing, poet. So, so, lift the cup higher."

Anacreon was an ancient Greek poet who was said to have died by choking on a grape-stone.

Lollio laughed.

"Alas! Alas!" Isabella said. "It is too full of pity to be laughed at! How did he become mad? Can thou tell me?"

Lollio answered, "For love, mistress. He was a pretty — an artful — poet, too, and that set him forwards on the road to madness first; the Muses then forsook him, he ran mad for a chambermaid, yet she was only a dwarf at that."

Lunatics, lovers, and poets are either out of touch with reality or in touch with a different kind of reality.

Franciscus said:

"Hail, bright Titania! Why stand thou idle on these flowery banks? Oberon is dancing with his dryads."

Oberon and Titania are the King and Queen of the Fairies.

Dryads are wood-nymphs.

In an attempt to seduce Isabella, Franciscus was saying that her husband was dancing — having affairs — with other women.

Franciscus continued:

"I'll gather daisies, primrose, violets, and bind them in a verse of poesy."

Lollio showed him a whip and said, "Not too near. You see your danger."

"Oh, hold thy hand, great Diomed!" Franciscus said. "Thou feed thy horses well. They shall obey thee. Get up on me and mount me; Bucephalus kneels."

Diomed of Thrace fed human flesh to his horses.

"Get up on me and mount me" has a sexual meaning.

Bucephalus was Alexander the Great's horse; only he could ride it.

Franciscus got down on all fours.

"You see how I awe my flock?" Lollio said. "A shepherd's dog is not more obedient."

"His conscience — his grasp of reality — is unquiet," Isabella said. "Surely that was the cause of this. He is a proper gentleman."

"Come here, Aesculapius. Hide the poison," Franciscus said.

Aesculapius is the ancient Greek god of medicine.

Lollio hid his whip and said, "Well, it is hidden."

Franciscus stood up and said, "Haven't thou ever heard about a man named Tiresias, a famous poet?"

Tiresias was a Theban soothsayer. He was once turned into a woman. After seven years as a woman, he became a man again. After having experienced sex as a man and as a woman, he said that women experienced more pleasure during sex than men. Angry, Juno, Queen of the gods, then struck him blind.

"Yes, he kept tame wild-geese," Lollio said.

In other words, he frequented prostitutes.

"That's him," Franciscus said. "I am the man."

"No," Lollio said.

"Yes, but make no words about it," Franciscus said. "I was a man seven years ago."

"A stripling, I think you might have been," Lollio said.

"Now I'm a woman, all feminine," Franciscus said.

"I wish that I might see that," Lollio said.

He wanted to see Franciscus naked.

"Juno struck me blind," Franciscus said.

"I'll never believe that," Lollio said. "For a woman, they say, has an eye more than a man."

Hmm.

That "eye" is a vagina.

"I say she struck me blind," Franciscus said.

"And Luna made you mad," Lollio said. "You have two trades to beg with."

He could beg for alms as a blind man and as a lunatic.

Franciscus said:

"Luna is now big-bellied, and there's room for both of us to ride with Hecate. I'll drag thee up into her silver sphere, and there we'll kick the dog and beat the bush that barks against the witches of the night."

Luna is the goddess of the Moon. "Big-bellied" means 1) pregnant, and 2) full, as in a full Moon.

Hecate is one part of a tripartite goddess: a goddess with three forms. In Heaven, the goddess is Luna, goddess of the Moon. On Earth, the goddess is Diana (Roman name) and Artemis (Greek name), goddess of the hunt. In Hell, the goddess is Hecate, goddess of witchcraft.

Hecate is a woman, and so is Isabella. Franciscus and Lollio could ride with Hecate. It sounded as if Franciscus wanted a threesome with Isabella and Lollio.

The Man in the Moon had a lantern, a thornbush, and a dog.

The dog barks, not the bush, but these are words that belong to a madman.

The dog can be likened to a shepherd's dog that protects the sheep. Isabella is the sheep, and Francesco does not want her protected from him, and so he wanted to kick the dog. The dog may be Alibius.

After beating Alibius, Francesco and Lollio can sexually beat — pummel — the bushy vulva of Isabella, who has been resisting the witches of the night. One such "witch" is Venus, the goddess of sexual passion. Another such witch may be Medea.

Franciscus continued:

"The swift lycanthropi that walk the rounds like watchmen do, we'll tear their wolvish skins, and save the sheep."

Lycanthropi are madmen who think that they are wolves.

Lollio was one of the lycanthropi. He was supposed to be protecting Isabella, but he wanted to sleep with her. Of course, so did Franciscus. Getting rid of the watchman looking over Isabella would help Lollio and Franciscus to be able to sleep with her.

The watchman Franciscus means is probably Alibius, since Lollio would join Franciscus in tearing his wolfish hide.

In his attempt to seduce Isabella, Franciscus had hinted that her husband was dancing — having affairs — with other women, and so her husband had a wolfish hide. Franciscus was describing Alibius as having a cruel — wolvish — character.

But right now, Lollio was the watchman. He had taken over looking after the madmen for a while because Alibius was away from his home.

Franciscus beat Lollio.

"Has it come to this?" Lollio said. "Nay, then, my poison comes forth again! Mad slave, indeed, you physically abuse — you beat — your keeper?"

Lollio showed Franciscus the whip.

"I ask you to go away from here with him," Isabella said. "Now he grows dangerous."

Franciscus sang:

"*Sweet love, pity me.*

"*Give me leave [permission] to lie with thee.*"

Franciscus may be as ready to sleep with Lollio as he is to sleep with Isabella.

"No, I'll see you wiser first," Lollio said to Franciscus. "Go to your own kennel."

"No noise, she sleeps, draw all the curtains round," Franciscus said. "Let no soft sound molest the pretty soul except love, and love creeps in at a mousehole."

Who is the "she" Franciscus was referring to? Possibly himself. Franciscus appeared to be bisexual.

A "mouse" is a beloved woman, and a "hole" is a vagina.

Lollio said:

"I wish you would get into your hole."

Franciscus exited to take a nap.

Lollio then said:

"Now, mistress, I will bring you another sort; you shall be fool another while."

He said loudly:

"Tony, come hither, Tony, look who's yonder, Tony.

Antonio entered the scene.

Antonio asked Lollio, "Cousin, isn't this my aunt?"

One meaning of "aunt" is "whore."

"Yes, it is one of them, Tony," Lollio said.

Antonio said to Lollio, "He, he, how do you do, uncle?"

If an "aunt" is a whore, then an "uncle" may be a pimp.

"Don't be afraid of him, mistress," Lollio said. "He is a gentle nidget — a gentle fool. You may play with him as safely as with his bauble."

A "bauble" can be 1) a court jester's (Fool's) baton, 2) a toy or trinket, or 3) a penis.

"How long have thou been a fool?" Isabella asked Antonio.

"Ever since I came here, cousin," Antonio said.

"Cousin?" Isabella said. "I'm not one of thy cousins, fool."

One meaning of "cousin" is "prostitute." Another meaning is the victim of a conman.

"Oh, mistress, fools have always so much wit as to claim their kindred," Lollio said.

In other words: Fools are intelligent enough to recognize other fools.

A madman in the inner chamber shouted, "Bounce! Bounce! He falls! He falls!"

"Bounce!" may mean "bang!" — the sound of a gun or an explosion.

"Listen, your scholars in the upper room are out of order," Isabella said.

Lollio shouted to the noisy madman:

"Must I come among you there?"

He then said to Isabella:

"Take care of the fool named Tony, mistress. I'll go up and play left-handed Orlando among the madmen."

Ariosto's *Orlando Furioso* is about the furious warrior Orlando, who suffered a fit of madness.

Lollio will play the part left-handed, which may mean poorly.

Lollio exited.

Immediately, Antonio stopped looking and acting like a fool.

"Well, sir," Isabella said, noticing the change.

"It is an opportune time now, sweet lady!" Antonio said. "Nay, cast no amazed eye upon this change of looks and behavior."

"Ha!" Isabella said.

Antonio said, "This guise of folly shrouds and covers your dearest love, the truest servant to your powerful beauties, whose magic had this force thus to transform me."

In other words, he had been pretending to be a fool so that he could get close to Isabella and seduce her.

"You are a fine fool indeed," Isabella said.

"Oh, it is not strange," Antonio said, "Love has an intellect that runs through all the scrutinizing sciences and, like a cunning and artful poet, catches a quantity of every knowledge, yet brings all home into one mystery, into one secret that he proceeds in."

A "mystery" is "a skill that requires much knowledge to practice."

"You are a dangerously cunning fool," Isabella said.

"There is no danger in me," Antonio said. "I bring nothing but love and his soft, wounding shafts to strike you with. Try but one arrow; if it hurt you, I'll stand you twenty back in recompense."

"Shafts" can be erections, but Antonio's shaft may be, as he says it is, soft. That would explain why he says to Isabella, "There is no danger in me."

But chances are, his shaft would soon cease being soft.

Possibly, "soft, wounding shafts" are kisses.

"Arrows" can be erections.

"Stand" means "give you back."

A "stand" is also an erection, and so "stand you twenty back in recompense" means "have sex with you twenty more times in recompense."

"You are a forward fool, too," Isabella said.

"This was Love's teaching," Antonio said. "A thousand ways the god of Love — Cupid — fashioned for me to find my way to you, and this I found the safest and nearest way to tread the Galaxia — the Milky Way — to my star."

"Tread" has a sexual meaning: to have sex.

"Milk" is a whitish fluid. Antonio would like a whitish fluid to pass from him to Isabella.

According to the *Oxford English Dictionary*, a "star" is "Perhaps: a crack or fissure in the skin."

Antonio's star is Isabella's vulva.

Isabella said, "You are also a profound fool. Certainly, you dreamt of this. Love never taught it to you when you were awake."

"Take no acquaintance — no notice — of these outward follies," Antonio said. "There is within this disguise a gentleman who loves you."

Isabella said:

"When I see him, I'll speak with him, so in the meantime keep your habit — your fool's costume. It becomes you well enough.

"As you are a gentleman, I'll not reveal who you are. That's all the favor that you must expect."

Isabella was saying that Antonio must not expect sexual favors.

Isabella continued:

"When you are weary of this play-acting, you may leave the school of fools, for all this while you have only played the fool."

Lollio returned.

Antonio said to Isabella:

"And I must play the fool again."

He resumed his acting and said to Isabella:

"He, he, I thank you, cousin. I'll be your valentine tomorrow morning."

Lollio asked Isabella, "How do you like the fool, mistress?"

"Surpassingly well, sir," Isabella said.

"Isn't he witty, pretty well for a fool?" Lollio said.

"If he continues on as he begins, he is likely to come to something!" Isabella said.

The verb "come" can mean "cum."

A "thing" is a sex organ; it can be male or female.

Lollio said:

"Aye, thank a good tutor. You may put him to it; he begins to answer pretty hard questions."

"Put him to it" has a sexual meaning, and it also means "test him."

"Put to" can mean "insert penis."

Lollio then asked:

"Tony, how many is five times six?"

"Five times six is six times five," Antonio said.

Lollio said to Isabella:

"What arithmetician could have answered better?"

He then asked Antonio:

"How many is one hundred and seven?"

"One hundred and seven is seven hundred and one, cousin," Antonio said.

Lollio said:

"This is no wit to speak about."

He asked Isabella:

"Will you be rid of the fool now?"

"By no means," Isabella said. "Let him stay a little while."

A madman in the inner chamber shouted, "Catch there! Catch the last couple in hell!"

Barley-break is a running-and-chasing game played by three couples. The couple in Hell — the middle ground — tried to catch the two other couples as they ran through Hell.

The madman's words can be understood as a warning.

"Again?" Lollio said. "Must I come among you? I wish that my master were home again! I am not able to govern both these wards — the fools' ward and the madmen's ward — together."

Lollio exited.

Again dropping the pretense of being a fool, Antonio asked Isabella, "Why should a minute of love's hour be lost?"

"Bah! Out of character again!" Isabella said. "I prefer that you keep your other posture: You do not become your tongue when you speak differently from your clothes."

According to Isabella, Antonio spoke more becomingly when he spoke in the character of a fool rather than in the character of a lover. Right now, he was wearing the clothing of a fool.

Antonio said, "How can a man freeze who lives near so sweet a warmth? Shall I alone walk through the orchard of the Hesperides and cowardly not dare to pull — to pluck — an apple from a branch? This with the red cheeks I must venture for."

The orchard of the Hesperides grew golden apples.

This society called the color of gold "red."

The apple Antonio wanted to pick may be likened to the fruit of the Tree of Knowledge of Good and Evil.

The "apple" with the red cheeks was also Isabella.

Lollio returned. He was in a high vantage point, and Antonio did not see him.

"Take heed, there are giants who keep them," Isabella said.

Isabella may have noticed Lollio watching them. Lollio may be a big or fat man: a giant.

An actor who played the role of Lollio was fat: William Rowley, co-author of *The Changeling*.

A snake (or dragon) named Ladon guarded the golden apples. It was the offspring of the giant Tython.

Antonio kissed Isabella.

Lollio said to himself:

"What is this now, fool? Are you good at that? Have you read Lipsius?"

Lipsius was a Renaissance scholar.

Lollio continued saying to himself:

"He's past *Ars Amandi*. I believe I must put harder questions to him. I perceive that."

Ovid wrote *Ars Amandi*, aka *The Art of Loving*. It is a treatise on techniques of seduction.

"You are bold without fear, too," Isabella said.

Antonio said:

"What should I fear, having all joys around me?

"If you smile, love shall play the wanton on your lip. Lips shall meet and retire, retire and meet again in kisses.

"Just look at me cheerfully, and in your eyes, I shall behold my own deformity, and dress myself up fairer. I know this disguise of fool does not become me, but in those bright mirrors of your eyes I shall array myself handsomely."

Lollio said to himself, "Cuckoo! Cuckoo!"

Lollio was certain that Alibius was soon to become a cuckold.

Lollio exited.

Some madmen took his place on the high vantage point.

Some of the madmen made the sounds of birds, and the others made the sounds of beasts.

Antonio and Isabella looked up at them.

"Who are these?" Antonio asked.

Isabella said:

"They are frightening enough to part us, yet they are only our schools of lunatics, who act their fantasies and delusions in any shapes and disguises suiting their immediate thoughts without first engaging in rational thinking.

"If they are sad, they cry. If mirth is their conceit and mood, they laugh again. Sometimes they imitate the beasts and birds, singing or howling, braying, barking. They all act as their wild fancies prompt them."

The madmen exited.

Lollio walked over to Antonio and Isabella.

"These are no fears," Antonio said.

"But here's a large one," Isabella said. "My serving-man."

Lollio may be a big or fat man.

"Ha, he, that's fine entertainment indeed, cousin," Antonio said to Lollio.

Lollio said:

"I wish that my master had come home. It is too much for one shepherd to govern two of these flocks. Nor can I believe that one churchman can instruct two benefices at once. There will be some incurable mad on the one side and complete fools on the other."

Some priests held more than one benefice: They were responsible for serving more than one church. This increased their income, but it lessened the amount of service the priest could give to a benefice.

Lollio then said:

"Come, Tony."

"Please, cousin, let me stay here still," Antonio said.

"No, you must go to your book now," Lollio said. "You have played sufficiently long."

"Your fool has grown wondrously witty," Isabella said.

"Well, I'll say nothing," Lollio said, "but I don't think anything except that he will put you down one of these days."

In other words: Lollio expects Antonio to lay Isabella down in bed.

"Put you down" also means "outwit you."

Lollio and Antonio exited.

Isabella said:

"Here the restrained current might make breach, in spite of the watchful bankers."

Bankers repaired the washed-out banks of streams and rivers.

The banks may metaphorically be the lips of Isabella's vulva.

Or they may be Alibius and Lollio, who either want Isabella to not commit adultery (Alibius) or who are supposed to not want Isabella to commit adultery (Lollio).

Isabella may have been growing wet with desire with Antonio.

Isabella continued:

"If a woman would stray and commit adultery, she need not gad abroad — outside her home — to seek her sin. It would be brought home and accomplished one way or other. The needle's point will move to the fixed north. Such drawing arctics — magnetic poles — women's beauties are."

A needle's point — a penis — is drawn to a beautiful woman, and so a beautiful woman who wants to commit adultery can readily find opportunities to do so.

Lollio returned and asked Isabella, "How are thou, sweet rogue?"

"How are things now?" Isabella asked.

"Come, there are degrees of rank," Lollio said. "One fool may be better than another."

"What's the matter?" Isabella asked.

"Nay, if thou give thy mind to fools, flesh, have at thee!" Lollio said.

"Have at thee!" means "Here I come!" In this society, a man would say that before attacking his opponent in a duel.

He tried to kiss her.

"You bold slave, you!" Isabella said.

Lollio said:

"I could follow now as the other fool did."

He imitated Antonio and quoted him word for word:

"What should I fear, having all joys about me?

"Just look at me cheerfully, and in your eyes, I shall behold my own deformity, and dress myself up fairer. I know this disguise of fool does not become me, but in those bright mirrors of your eyes I shall array myself handsomely."

Lollio then said:

"And so as it follows.

"But isn't that way the more foolish way?"

Lollio preferred the direct approach.

He continued:

"Come, sweet rogue, kiss me, my little Lacedaemon."

Helen was the Queen of Sparta, which is in Lacedaemon. She went either willingly or unwillingly with Paris to Troy and so became Helen of Troy. Menelaus (her legitimate husband) and many other Greeks fought a war against Troy.

"Lacedaemon" may be wordplay meaning "laced mutton." "Mutton" is a slang word for "prostitute," so "my little Lacedaemon" would be "my little lace-wearing whore."

"Laced" can mean "ensnared." Lollio thinks that he has ensnared her by eavesdropping on her conversation with Antonio and seeing Antonio kiss her.

The Spartans were known for speaking tersely. Isabella would not tell Lollio words that he would like to hear.

Lollio continued:

"Let me feel how thy pulses beat. Thou have a thing about thee that would do a man pleasure. I'll lay my hand on it."

That thing was between her legs.

Isabella said:

"Sirrah, no more! I see you have discovered this love's knight-errant, who has made adventure for purchase of my love."

Antonio was love's knight-errant, who had risked a lot to win Isabella's love — or at least her willingness to engage in sex with him.

Isabella continued:

"Be silent, mute, mute as a statue, or his injunction for enjoying sex with me shall be to cut thy throat.

"I'll do it, although for no other purpose, and we can be sure he'll not refuse it."

Isabella was threatening Lollio: Either he keeps his mouth shut about her, or she will tell Antonio to cut Lollio's throat, with Antonio's reward being to sleep with her.

"My share, that's all I want," Lollio said. "I'll have my fool's part with you."

He wanted to sleep with her.

"No more," Isabella said. "Your master is coming!"

Alibius entered the scene.

"Sweet, how are thou doing?" Alibius asked Isabella.

"I am your bound servant, sir," Isabella replied.

She was "duty-bound" to Alibius, and she was imprisoned in their home.

Alibius said, "Bah, bah, sweetheart, no more of that."

"It would be best for you to lock me up," Isabella said.

A chastity belt would keep her safe from people such as Lollio.

Alibius replied:

"In my arms and bosom, my sweet Isabella, I'll lock thee up most nearly."

"Most nearly" means 1) most intimately, and 2) most like a lock.

Alibius then said:

"Lollio, we have employment; we have a task in hand.

"At noble Vermandero's, our castle-captain's, there is a nuptial to be solemnized. Beatrice Joanna, his fair daughter, will be the bride.

"For this nuptial, the gentleman has commissioned us. He wants a mixture of our madmen and our fools to finish, as it were, and make the fag-end of all the revels on the third night from the first."

The wedding celebrations would last three days. The madmen and fools would appear at the very end.

Alibius then said:

"They are supposed only to make an unexpected passage over the ballroom floor to cause a pleasant fright in the guests, that is all.

"But that is not all I aim to do.

"If we could teach the madmen and fools to make their passage over the ballroom floor in a wild, distracted measure and dance, although not in accordance with the usual form and figure, breaking time's head by not dancing in time to the music, it wouldn't matter."

"Breaking time's head" may mean "breaking time's maidenhead." By dancing badly, the madmen and fools would be violently assaulting time.

If time were metaphorically cuckolded by this dance, then a cuckold's horns would break out on time's head.

Alibius continued:

"Time's head would be healed again in one age or other, if not in this."

With more time and practice, Alibius and Lollio could teach the madmen and fools to dance better. The dance could still be done in a wild, distracted measure in order to pleasurably frighten the guests, but it would be done in time to the music.

Alibius continued:

"This, this, Lollio."

He showed Lollio money, and then he added:

"There's a good reward begun, and it will beget a bounty, let me tell you."

If they could teach the madmen and fools to put on a good dance performance, they could make much money. The "bounty" may be an extra tip.

"This is easy, sir, I'll guarantee you that," Lollio said. "You have about you fools and madmen who can dance very well, and it is no wonder that your best dancers are not the wisest men. The reason is that with frequent jumping, they jolt their brains down into their feet, with the result that their wits lie more in their heels than in their heads."

"Honest Lollio, thou give me a good reason for believing you and there is a comfort in it," Alibius said.

"You have a fine business of it," Isabella said. "Madmen and fools are a staple — a basic — commodity."

Money can be made from madmen and fools.

Alibius said:

"Oh, wife, we must eat, wear clothes, and live.

"Just at the lawyer's haven we arrive.

"By madmen and by fools, we both do thrive."

They made their living from madmen and fools.

According to cynics, madmen and fools frequent lawyers' offices. They are a haven for lawyers because lawyers make money from them.

People would also go to lawyers' offices when they wanted to control a madman's or a fool's estate on the grounds that the madman or the fool was incapable of handling their affairs.

Vermandero, Alsemero, Jasperino, and Beatrice talked together in a chamber in the castle. Vermandero was Beatrice's father.

Vermandero said to Alsemero, "The town of Valencia speaks so nobly of you, sir. I wish I had a daughter now for you."

Alsemero said about Beatrice, "The fellow of this creature would be a partner for a king's love."

The "fellow" would be a metaphorical or actual twin.

Vermandero said:

"I had her fellow once, sir, but Heaven has married her to joys eternal. It would be a sin to wish her in this vale of tears again."

The "fellow" could be a wife or a daughter who had died.

Vermandero continued:

"Come, sir, your friend and you shall see the pleasures that my health chiefly enjoys."

"I hear the beauty of this seat — this castle — much praised everywhere I go," Alsemero said.

"It falls much short of that," Vermandero said.

Everyone except Beatrice exited.

She said:

"So, here's one step Alsemero has made into my father's favor; time will make him a fixture here. I have got him now the liberty of the house.

"So wisdom by degrees works out her freedom. And if that eye be darkened that offends me — I wait but that eclipse — this gentleman shall soon shine glorious in my father's liking, through the refulgent — resplendently reflecting — virtue of my love."

The eye that offended her was that of Alonzo. She wanted that eye darkened — dead.

Matthew 18:9 states, "*And if your eye causes you to stumble, gouge it out and throw it away. It is better for you to enter life with one eye than to have two eyes and be thrown into the fire of hell*" (King James Version).

Deflores entered the scene. He expected to be rewarded with sex for his murder of Alonzo.

Deflores said to himself:

"My thoughts are at a banquet for the deed."

After committing the murder, he was in a festive mood: He was looking forward to having sex with Beatrice.

Deflores continued:

"I feel no weight from doing the deed; it is only light and cheap compared to the sweet recompense that I set and specified in exchange for it."

He felt no guilt from committing the act of murder; he felt only anticipation for having sex with Beatrice.

"Deflores," Beatrice said.

"Lady," Deflores said.

"Thy looks cheerfully promise good news," Beatrice said.

"All things are answerable and fitting for our purposes: time, circumstance, your wishes, and my service," Deflores said.

"Is it done then?" Beatrice asked.

"Piracquo is no more," Deflores said about Alonzo.

"My joys start at my eyes," Beatrice said. "Our sweetest delights are forevermore born weeping."

"I've a token for you," Deflores said.

The token was evidence that he had committed the murder, and it was a love-token from him to her.

"For me?" Beatrice asked.

Deflores showed her Alonzo's finger and diamond ring.

"But it was sent somewhat unwillingly," Deflores said. "I could not get the ring without the finger."

"Bless me!" Beatrice said. "What have thou done?"

"Why, is that more than killing the whole man?" Deflores said. "I cut his heartstrings. A greedy hand thrust in a dish at court in a mistake has had as much as this."

The greedy hand could have a finger cut off by mistake by another diner's knife.

A finger can be thrust into a dish, and a penis can be thrust into a woman.

"It is the first token my father made me send him," Beatrice said about the diamond ring.

"And I made him send it back again for his last token. I was loathe to leave it," Deflores said. "And I'm sure dead men have no use of jewels. He was as loath to part with it, for it stuck as if the flesh and it were both one substance."

"Jewels" are metaphorical maidenheads and/or testicles.

Beatrice and Alonzo had been betrothed.

Matthew 19:4-5 (King James Version) states:

4 "Haven't you read," he replied, "that at the beginning the Creator 'made them male and female,'

5 and said, 'For this reason a man will leave his father and mother and be united to his wife, and the two will become one flesh'?

Beatrice said:

"At the stag's fall, the game-keeper has his fees. It is soon applied. All dead men's fees are yours, sir."

The game-keeper would be awarded part of the kill.

Beatrice continued:

"Please bury the finger, but the stone — the diamond — you may make use of shortly; the true value, take it from me as my truth, is almost three hundred ducats."

Beatrice's "truth" is also her chastity: something that Deflores wants to take from her.

Deflores said:

"It will hardly buy a capcase — a traveling bag — for one's conscience, though, to keep it away from the worm of remorse, as fine as it is."

Mark 9:47-48 (King James Version) states:

47 And if your eye causes you to stumble, pluck it out. It is better for you to enter the kingdom of God with one eye than to have two eyes and be thrown into hell,

48 where 'the worms that eat them do not die, and the fire is not quenched.'

Deflores continued:

"Well, since it is my fees, I'll take it. Great men have taught me that, or else my merit — my sense of what I deserve — would scorn the way of it — this way of rewarding me."

Great men have taught Deflores to accept money as recompense, so he accepted it reluctantly. He believed that sex with Beatrice was his true reward, and he believed that that reward was coming to him.

Beatrice said:

"It might justly, sir."

She thought that Deflores was reluctant to accept the diamond ring because it was not of enough value, but Beatrice knew that it was not supposed to be his fee. It was something in addition to the fee.

Beatrice said:

"Why, thou are mistaken, Deflores. It is not given to you by way of recompense."

"No, I hope not, lady," Deflores said. "You should soon witness my contempt for it then."

"Please, thou look as if thou were offended," Beatrice said.

Deflores said, "That recompense — the diamond ring — would be strange, lady; it is not possible that my service should draw such a reproach from you. Offended? Could you think such would be my recompense? That would be 'much' for one of my performance, and so warm yet in my service."

Deflores was thinking of sex. He had performed the killing of Alonzo, and now he wanted to perform in the bedroom.

"It would be misery in me to give you a reproach, sir," Beatrice said.

In other words: Criticizing Deflores would cause her misery.

Deflores said:

"I know so much."

If she were to criticize him after he had committed murder for her, he would make her miserable.

Deflores continued:

"It would be so — misery in her sharpest condition."

"Our misunderstanding is resolved then," Beatrice said, misunderstanding him. "Look, sir, here's three thousand golden florins. I have not meanly and ungenerously thought upon thy merit: what thou deserve."

"What! Salary! Financial reward!" Deflores said. "Now you move and anger me!"

"What!" Beatrice said. "Deflores!"

"Do you place me in the rank of verminous fellows who destroy things for wages?" Deflores said. "Do you offer me gold? For the lifeblood of man! Is anything valued too precious for my recompense?"

He did not want money. He wanted sex.

"I don't understand thee," Beatrice said.

Deflores said, "I could have hired a journeyman in murder — a paid assassin — at this rate, and I might have my own conscience and might have had the work brought home!"

The murder would have been easily done — brought home — by a paid assassin, and Deflores would have had the satisfaction of knowing that his own hands had not committed the murder. Deflores could have stayed at home and the assassin would have brought him the news that the murder had been committed.

Deflores' conscience would not have bothered him, but the conscience of another man may have bothered that man.

Beatrice said to herself:

"I'm in a labyrinth. What will content him and make him happy? I am eager to be rid of him."

Beatrice said out loud:

"I'll double the sum, sir."

"You are taking a course of action that will double my vexation," Deflores said. "That's all the good you do."

Beatrice said to herself:

"Bless me! I am now in a worse plight than I was. I don't know what will please him."

She said out loud:

"For my fear's sake, I beg you to make your escape and go away with all possible speed. And if thou are so modest not to name the sum that will content thee, paper does not blush.

"Send thy demand in writing; the amount you demand shall follow thee.

"But please take thy flight."

"You must flee, too, then," Deflores said.

He wanted her to go with him.

"I?" Beatrice asked.

"I'll not stir a foot else," Deflores said.

"What do you mean?" Beatrice asked.

"Why, aren't you as guilty as I, and aren't you in, I'm sure, as deep as I? And we should stick together. Come, your fears counsel you but ill: Your fears give you bad advice. My absence would draw suspicion upon you instantly. There would be no rescue for you."

Deflores had hidden Alonzo's corpse. As long as it were not found, people might think that Alonzo had jilted Beatrice and left the palace.

If Deflores were to flee now, questions would be asked about Alonzo's disappearance.

"He speaks home," Beatrice said to herself. "He says the truth. I am guilty and in danger."

Deflores said, "Nor is it fitting that we two who are engaged so jointly should part and live asunder."

They were joint partners in the crime, and the word "engaged" calls to mind the meaning of "betrothed."

Deflores tried to kiss her.

"What is this now, sir?" Beatrice said. "This shows not well on you."

Deflores was from a lower social class than Beatrice.

"What makes — why is — your lip so strange and unfriendly?" Deflores said. "This strangeness must not be between us."

Beatrice said to herself, "The man talks wildly."

"Come, kiss me with a zeal now!" Deflores said.

Beatrice said to herself, "Heaven, I fear him!"

Deflores said, "I will not stand so long to beg for your kisses, soon."

He thought that soon he would have many kisses from her.

"Take heed, Deflores, of forgetfulness," Beatrice said. "It will soon betray us."

If someone were to see Deflores kissing her, that someone might suspect that Deflores had committed the murder of Alonzo. That person also might suspect that Beatrice had helped plan the murder.

"You take heed first," Deflores said. "Indeed, you are grown much forgetful of your guilt. You are too blameworthy in it."

Deflores thought that Beatrice was forgetful of her obligation to him and of her own guilt in the murder.

Beatrice said, "He's sexually bold, and I am blamed for it."

Deflores said, "I have eased you of your trouble; think about that. I'm in pain and I must be eased by you. It is a charity. Justice invites your blood — your sexuality — to understand me."

Deflores' pain was sexual deprivation, and Beatrice could ease that pain by having sex with him.

"I dare not," Beatrice said.

"Quickly," Deflores said.

Beatrice said, "Oh, I never shall! Speak it yet further off so that I may lose and forget what has been spoken, and no sound remain of it! I would not hear so much offensive language again for such another deed."

The deed was another act of murder.

Deflores said:

"Hold on, lady, hold on. The last part of your debt to me is not yet paid.

"Oh, this act of murder has put me into spirit: It has made my desire for sex swell up.

"I was as greedy for it as the parched earth is greedy for moisture when the clouds weep."

Deflores' swelled-up penis was greedy for moisture.

Deflores continued:

"Didn't you see how I worked to be given the task of serving you? Indeed, I sued for it and knelt for it? Why did I take all those pains?

"You see I have thrown contempt upon your gold, not that I don't want and need it, for I do piteously. In due course I will come to it and make use of it. But it was not held so precious to begin with, for I place wealth after the heels of sexual pleasure.

"And were I not certain that thy virginity were perfect in thee, I should take my recompense only with grudging, as if I had but half my hopes I agreed for."

Beatrice said:

"Why, it is impossible thou can be so wicked, or shelter such a cunning cruelty, as to make Alonzo's death the murderer of my honor!"

Her honor was her reputation for chastity. She did not want Deflores to take her virginity.

Beatrice continued:

"Thy language is so bold and vicious that I cannot see which way I can forgive it with any modesty.

"Bah, you forget yourself," Deflores said. "A woman dipped in blood and talk of modesty!"

In other words: A woman who has arranged to have a man murdered should not have qualms about giving up her virginity.

"Oh, misery of sin!" Beatrice said. "I wish that I had been bound perpetually to my living hate in that Piracquo rather than to hear these words! Think but upon the distance that creation set between thy blood and mine, and keep thee there."

Their social ranks were different. Beatrice's social rank was higher than that of Deflores. She wanted him to know his place, and to stay there.

Deflores said:

"Just look into your conscience and read me there. It is a true book; you'll find me there your equal.

"Bah, don't flee to your birth, but settle on what the act has made you; you are no more than a murderer now. You must forget your parentage when it comes to me and not hold your high birth over me. You are the creature of your deeds: Your deeds make you who you are.

"By that name of murderer, you lost your first condition, your original innocence, and I lay claim to you, as peace and innocence have turned you out of Paradise and made you one with me. We are now equals."

Beatrice's birth and social rank may be higher than that of Deflores, but her deeds have made her character the equal of Deflores' character. Both were equal in evil.

Beatrice had been banned from at least the Earthly Paradise: the Garden of Eden.

"With thee, foul villain?" Beatrice said.

Deflores replied:

"Yes, my fair murderess. Do you provoke me?"

Now Deflores stopped addressing Beatrice with the respectful "you" and instead addressed her with the less respectful "thou":

"Although thou claim that thou are a maiden and a virgin, thou are a whore in thy sexual desire. The object of your sexual desire was changed from thy first love to thy second love, and that's a kind of whoredom in thy heart; and thy first love's changed now from living to dead to bring thy second love on.

"Thy second love is thy Alsemero, and by all sweets that ever darkness tasted, if I do not sexually enjoy thee, thou will never sexually enjoy him. I'll blast the hopes and joys of thy marriage. I'll confess everything. My life I rate and value at nothing."

Beatrice said, "Deflores!"

Deflores said:

"I shall rest from all lovers' plagues then."

With his death, he will not feel love's plagues.

Deflores continued:

"I live in pain now: That shooting eye will burn my heart to cinders."

Deflores was in sexual pain because of Beatrice's eyes that shot glances.

"Oh, sir, listen to me!" Beatrice said.

"She who in life and love refuses me, in death and shame she shall be my partner," Deflores said.

If she did not have sex with him, he would ruin her reputation and take her life.

Beatrice knelt and said:

"Wait, hear me once and for all."

"I make thee master of all the wealth I have in gold and jewels. Let me go poor to my bed with honor, and I am rich in all things."

Deflores said, "Let this silence thee: The wealth of all Valencia shall not buy my sexual pleasure from me. Can you weep fate from its determined purpose? So soon may you weep me from my determined purpose."

In other words: What is fated to happen will happen. Deflores' determination to sleep with Beatrice was like fate.

"Vengeance begins," Beatrice said. "Murder, I see, is followed by more sins. Was my creation in the womb so cursed that it must engender with a viper first?"

The viper was Deflores. He was demanding that she sleep with him before she could sleep with Alsemero.

Deflores said:

"Come, rise and shroud — hide — your blushes in my bosom. Silence is one of pleasure's best receipts."

Beatrice rose.

Deflores would receive sexual pleasure in exchange for his silence. Silence was being given for sexual pleasure.

Deflores continued:

"Thy peace is wrought forever in this yielding. Alas, how the turtledove pants! Thou shall love soon what thou so fear and faint to venture on."

Deflores was certain that soon Beatrice would learn to enjoy having sex with him.

[Dumb Show]

Some gentlemen entered the scene, and Vermandero met them. He pantomimed wonder at the flight of Alonzo de Piracquo.

Alsemero entered the scene, accompanied by Jasperino and some gallants. Vermandero pointed to Alsemero, and the gentlemen made motions that showed approval of his choice of Alsemero to be Beatrice's husband.

Vermandero exited, followed in a procession by Alsemero, Jasperino, and the gentlemen and gallants.

Beatrice the bride entered the scene in great state and pomp, accompanied by Diaphanta, Isabella, and other gentlewomen.

Deflores entered after all the women, and he smiled at the occasion.

Alonzo's Ghost appeared to Deflores in the midst of his smile and startled him, showing him the hand whose finger he had cut off.

All exited with great ceremoniousness.

Alsemero and Beatrice were now married.

CHAPTER 4

— 4.1 —

Beatrice was in Alsemero's private chamber.

Alone, she said to herself:

"This fellow has undone me endlessly."

The fellow was Deflores, who had been having lots of sex with Beatrice. This had ruined her for her wedding night with Alsemero because in this society, brides entering first marriages were supposed to be virgins. In addition to causing her much trouble, the act, if not confessed and repented, would condemn her to spend eternity in Hell.

Beatrice continued:

"Never was a bride so fearfully distressed. I think upon the ensuing wedding night, and whom I am to cope with in embraces —"

The word "cope" means "meet," but in this context it also suggests "copulate."

Beatrice continued:

"— one who is ennobled both in blood and mind, and is so clear in understanding. That's my plague now. Before Alsemero's judgment, my fault and lack of chastity will appear like malefactors' crimes before tribunals.

"There is no hiding it.

"The more I think upon the ensuing wedding night, and whom I am to cope with in embraces, the more I dive into my own distress."

Beatrice continued:

"How a wise man stands for a great calamity!"

To a guilty person, a meeting with a wise man results in calamity because the wise man will find the guilty person out. Wise men make good judges.

Beatrice continued:

"Whatsoever course of action I alight upon, there's no venturing into his bed, without my shame, which may grow up to danger."

She was worried that if she slept with her husband, he would know that she was not a virgin. This would make her ashamed, and he might become violent.

Beatrice continued:

"He cannot but in justice strangle me as I lie by (and lie to) him, and he will treat me like a cheater. It is a 'precious' — a risky — craft to play with a false die before a cunning gamester. Doing so takes rare skill."

"Die" is the singular of "dice."

Beatrice continued:

"Here's his closet."

A closet is a small room.

Beatrice continued:

"The key has been left in it, and he is abroad in the park."

The castle's park was a place for gentlemen to ride horses and hunt.

Beatrice continued:

"Surely the key was forgotten. I'll be so bold as to look in the closet."

She opened the door and said:

"Bless me! A true physician's closet it is, set round with vials of medicine; each one has its own label, too. Surely, he practices medicine for his own use, which may be safely called your great man's wisdom because it protects his health."

The great men of the world, such as kings, need to worry about being poisoned. And so it is wise for them to keep a supply of antidotes.

Beatrice continued:

"What manuscript lies here? *The Book of Experiment,* subtitled *Secrets in Nature.* So it is, it is so."

She read a passage from the Table of Contents out loud:

"*How to know whether a woman be with child or not.*"

Beatrice said to herself:

"I hope I am not pregnant yet — but if he should test me for pregnancy, though!"

She looked to see where the test for pregnancy was located in the book:

"Let me see. Folio [Page] forty-five."

She looked for that page and said:

"Here it is. The leaf is tucked down upon it; the place is suspicious."

She read out loud:

"*If you would know whether a woman is with child or not, give her two spoonfuls of the white water in glass C.*"

The "water" was a medicinal liquid.

Beatrice then asked herself:

"Where's that glass C? Oh, yonder I see it now."

A vial of the white water in Alsemero's closet.

Beatrice read out loud:

"*And if she is with child, she sleeps a full twelve hours after drinking the two spoonfuls; if she is not with child, she will not sleep a full twelve hours after drinking the two spoonfuls.*"

Beatrice said to herself:

"None of that water comes into my belly. I'll know you from a hundred: I can pick you out of a hundred vials. I could break you now or turn you into milk — that is, replace you with milk — and so beguile the master of the mystery [special medical knowledge], but I'll look out for you."

Alsemero would notice the broken vial, and the milk would spoil, but Beatrice could protect herself by pretending to drink the white water and dumping it out when her husband wasn't looking.

Beatrice continued talking to herself:

"Ha! That which comes next is ten times worse."

She read out loud:

"*How to know whether a woman is a maiden [virgin] or not.*"

She then said:

"If that test should be applied to me, what would become of me? Perhaps he has a strong faith in my purity — he has never yet made a test of it. But the author calls this —"

She read out loud:

"*A merry slight but true experiment. The author, Antonius Mizaldus. Give the party you suspect the quantity of a spoonful of the water in the glass M, which upon her who is a maiden makes three different effects: It will make her incontinently [immediately] yawn, then fall into a sudden sneezing, last into a violent laughing. Else, it will make her dull, heavy and sluggish, and lumpish.*"

"Else" in the final sentence is ambiguous:

1) "Thereafter, it will make her dull, heavy and sluggish, and lumpish."

2) "Otherwise [If she is not a maiden], it will make her dull, heavy and sluggish, and lumpish."

Both meanings, however, may be intended:

1) The virgin will yawn, sneeze, laugh, and then feel sad.

2) The non-virgin will not yawn, not sneeze, and not laugh, but will only feel sad.

Later, there is a reference to the potion having three effects on a virgin: yawning, sneezing, and laughing. In addition, however, the virgin who is tested later also becomes sad. And when another person is tested, she is expected to feel sadness if she is a virgin.

This pseudo-scientific test would not work, so ambiguity is desirable as it will help explain wrong results.

Beatrice said to herself:

"If I had not found this, what would have happened to me? I fear that my husband will test me, yet it is seven hours to bedtime. I have time to prepare myself in case my husband tries to test me."

Diaphanta, her serving-woman, entered the room.

"Cuds, madam, are you here?" Diaphanta asked.

"Cuds" means "May God save you [or me]." It is an oath.

Beatrice said to herself:

"Seeing that wench now, a trick comes in my mind.

"It is a nice piece — a scrupulously principled woman — whom gold cannot purchase."

She did not think that Diaphanta was such a woman.

She said to Diaphanta:

"I have come here, wench, to look for my lord."

Diaphanta said to herself:

"I wish I had such a reason to look for him, too. I wish that he were my husband."

She said to Beatrice:

"Why, he's in the park, madam."

"There let him be," Beatrice said.

Diaphanta said:

"Aye, madam, let him compass whole parks and forests, as great rangers do. At roosting time, a little lodge can hold them. Earth-conquering Alexander the Great, who thought the world too narrow for him, in the end had but his pit-hole."

Beatrice said, "I fear thou are not modest, Diaphanta."

Some of the words in Diaphanta's speech had a bawdy meaning.

"Compass" can mean "achieve a goal" in addition to "make a circuit of." "Rangers" are gamekeepers, but metaphorically they can be penises, "parks" may metaphorically mean vaginas, and "forests" can metaphorically mean female pubic hair.

At bedtime, a little vagina can lodge a penis.

The bawdy meaning of "pit-hole" is obvious. Its literal meaning is "grave." One meaning of "to die" is "to have an orgasm."

Diaphanta said, "Your thoughts are so unwilling to be known, madam. It is always the bride's custom towards bedtime to make light of her joys, as if she did not have them."

In other words: Your thoughts, and the thoughts of other brides, are also bawdy, although they do not customarily acknowledge that.

"Her joys?" Beatrice said. "Her fears, thou should say."

"Fear of what?" Diaphanta asked.

"Are thou a maiden, and talk so to a maiden?" Beatrice said. "You leave a blushing business behind, curse your heart for it. You make me blush."

The word "maiden" means "virgin."

The "blushing business" was that Diaphanta's words had made Beatrice blush, but "blushing business" can also mean sex, and so Beatrice perhaps was implying that Diaphanta may not be a virgin.

In fact, though, Diaphanta was a virgin, and she was looking forward to losing her virginity.

"Do you truly mean that, madam?" Diaphanta said. "Are you serious?"

"Well, if I'd thought upon the fear at first, Man should have been unknown to me," Beatrice said.

Her sentence was ambiguous.

One meaning of her sentence, intended for Diaphanta, was this: If I had thought about how afraid I am to lose my virginity, I would never have married Alsemero.

The other meaning of her sentence, intended for herself, was this: If I had thought about how afraid I would be that Alsemero would find out that I am not a virgin, I would never have had sex with Deflores.

"Is it possible?" Diaphanta said. "Are you serious?"

"I will give a thousand ducats to that woman who would experience what I am afraid of, and tell me the truth tomorrow when she gets away from it," Beatrice said. "If she likes it, I might perhaps be drawn to it."

"Are you in earnest?" Diaphanta said. "Are you serious?"

"Get the woman, then challenge me and see if I am serious, and see if I'll fly away from my promise and renege on it," Beatrice said, "but I must tell you this by the way, she must be a true maiden, or else there's no trial — my fears are not hers if she is not a virgin."

"Nay, the woman I would put into your hands, madam, shall be a maiden," Diaphanta said. "She shall be a virgin."

"You know I would be shamed if she were not a maiden," Beatrice said, "because she lies for me."

She would lie for Beatrice: 1) take her place in bed, and 2) enact an untruth by pretending to be Beatrice.

"This is a strange mood," Diaphanta said. "But are you serious still? Would you resign your first night's pleasure and give money, too?"

Beatrice said:

"As willingly as I wish to live."

Noting how eager and excited Diaphanta was, Beatrice said to herself:

"Alas, the gold is but a by-bet — a by-the-way part of the bet — to wedge in the honor."

Beatrice was making a bet that she could retain her honor by persuading Diaphanta to take her place on her — Beatrice's — wedding night. The gold was only a small part of the bet — a by-bet — because Beatrice was aware that Diaphanta wanted to sleep with Alsemero; Beatrice's "alas" showed that Beatrice was aware of that.

The money was an excuse for Diaphanta to agree to sleep with Alsemero without acknowledging that she wanted to sleep with Alsemero.

It is not a good idea to let a boss know that you want to sleep with her husband. It is better to let her think that you want the money. Beatrice was taking this into account and making sure that Diaphanta had an excuse to sleep with Beatrice's husband — an excuse that Diaphanta believed would not upset Beatrice.

The money would "wedge in the honor." It would tighten and make firmer Diaphanta's agreement to give up her honor by giving Beatrice an excuse for

Diaphanta to sleep with Alsemero that Diaphanta believed would not upset Beatrice. It would also allow Beatrice to retain a reputation for honesty. "Honor" can be wordplay for "on her," and Beatrice would allow Alsemero to be on Diaphanta.

Diaphanta said:

"I do not know how the world goes abroad for faith or honesty. Is there any faith and honesty in the world? There's both required in this."

Beatrice was showing neither faith nor honesty as a bride. She was bribing Diaphanta to sleep with her — Beatrice's — husband.

Diaphanta was also saying that she could not vouch for anyone else's faith and honesty. But she could vouch for her own. Why couldn't she be the maiden whom Beatrice is looking for?

Diaphanta continued:

"Madam, what do you say to me about sleeping with your husband? You need not stray any further and seek another person.

"I've a good mind, truly, to earn your money."

"You are too quick to volunteer, I fear, for you to be a maiden," Beatrice said.

The word "quick" can mean "pregnant."

"What! Not a maiden!" Diaphanta said. "Nay, then, you provoke me, madam, your honorable — your respectable and chaste — self is not a truer maiden with all your fears upon you —"

Beatrice, who was not a maiden, said to herself, "Bad enough then."

If Diaphanta were as true a virgin as Beatrice was, Diaphanta was no true virgin.

Diaphanta continued, "— than I with all my lightsome joys about me."

"I'm glad to hear it," Beatrice said. "Then you dare put your honesty upon an easy trial."

"Easy?" Diaphanta said. "Anything. Any trial."

Beatrice went inside her husband's closet and said, "I'll come back to you soon."

Diaphanta said, "She will not examine me, will she, like the forewoman of a female jury?"

In 1613, the Countess of Essex alleged that her marriage had not been consummated. As part of a divorce trial, she was physically examined by a group of matrons.

Beatrice picked up a vial and said to himself:

"Glass M. Aye, this is it."

She then said:

"Look, Diaphanta, You take no worse than I do."

She drank some of the liquid and handed Diaphanta the glass vial.

Diaphanta said, "And in so doing I will not question what it is, but take it."

She drank.

Beatrice said to herself:

"Now if the experiment is true, it will appraise and prove itself, and it will give me noble — splendid — ease."

Diaphanta yawned.

Beatrice continued saying to herself:

"Its effects begin already. There's the first symptom."

Diaphanta sneezed.

Beatrice continued saying to herself:

"And what haste it makes to fall into the second symptom, there by this time: Most admirable and wonderful secret! On the contrary, it stirs not me a whit, which it was most concerned to do."

The test had been intended for Beatrice, but the test gave the opposite result of what Alsemero had hoped for. It showed that Beatrice was not a maiden.

But the test showed that Diaphanta was indeed a maiden.

Diaphanta laughed, "Ha! Ha! Ha!"

Beatrice continued saying to herself:

"Precise in all things and in order, as if it were written down for Diaphanta to read and follow, one symptom gives way to another."

Diaphanta laughed, "Ha! Ha! Ha!"

"How are things now wench?" Beatrice asked.

Diaphanta said, "Ha! Ha! Ha! I am so, so light at heart! Ha! Ha! Ha! It is so pleasurable! Give me just one swig more, sweet madam."

"Aye, tomorrow," Beatrice said. "We shall have time to sit by it — sit and enjoy its effects."

She was pretending that she had felt the same joyfulness as Diaphanta.

"Now I'm sad again," Diaphanta said.

The instructions for the use of the vial had stated. "Else [Thereafter], it will make her dull, heavy and sluggish, and lumpish."

Beatrice said to herself:

"It lays itself and subsides so gently, too."

She then said out loud:

"Come, wench. Most honest — most virginal — Diaphanta I dare call thee now."

The test had shown that Diaphanta was a virgin.

"Please tell me, madam, what trick — what test — do you call this?" Diaphanta asked.

"I'll tell thee all hereafter," Beatrice said. "Now we must think about how we can carry out this business."

"I shall carry it out well because I love the burden," Diaphanta said.

In the missionary position, Alsemero would be a burden: He would be on top of her. Diaphanta would bear his weight.

Beatrice said, "About midnight you must not fail to steal from out of bed gently and quietly so that I may take your place."

Diaphanta said:

"Oh, don't worry about that, madam. I shall be cool and no longer sexually hot by that time.

"The bride's place, and with a thousand ducats!

"I'm for a justice now: I bring a portion with me. I scorn small fools!"

With a dowry of a thousand ducats, she could arrange a good marriage in front of a justice of the peace.

Diaphanta was also joking that with the dowry she need not settle for a little fool. The big fool whom she could marry could even be a justice of the peace.

They exited.

Vermandero and a servant talked together in a room in the castle.

Vermandero said:

"I tell thee, knave, my honor is in question. My honor is a thing until now free from suspicion, nor was there ever cause to suspect it."

If Alonzo had been murdered in Vermandero's castle, then even if Alonso's host, Vermandero, did not commit the murder, he would suffer a loss of honor because he had failed to provide a safe place for his guest.

Vermandero continued:

"Who of my gentlemen are absent? Tell me truly how many and who."

"Antonio, sir, and Franciscus," the servant answered.

"When did they leave the castle?" Vermandero asked.

"Some ten days ago, sir, the one intending to go to Briamata, the other intending to go to Valencia," the servant said.

Vermandero said:

"The time accuses them: an accusation of murder has been brought within my castle gate, Piracquo's murder. I cannot explain faithfully — with confidence — why Antonio and Franciscus are not here. A strict command of apprehension shall pursue them suddenly, and either wipe the stain off clear or openly reveal it.

"Provide for me winged warrants for the purpose of arresting them."

Tomazo de Piracquo entered the scene. He was the brother of the murdered Alonzo de Piracquo.

Seeing Tomazo, Vermandero said:

"See, I am set on and harassed again."

The servant exited to get the warrants for Antonio and Franciscus.

"I claim a brother of you," Tomazo said.

"You are too hot and angry," Vermandero said. "Don't seek him here."

"Yes, among your dearest bloods, your dearest relatives," Tomazo said. "If my peace of mind finds no fairer satisfaction, then this is the place that must yield account — satisfaction — for him, for here I left him, and the hasty tie of this snatched — this hasty — marriage gives strong testimony of his most certain ruin."

Beatrice and Alsemero were going to be married on this day, soon after the disappearance of Alonzo.

Tomazo thought that this was evidence that they had murdered Alonzo, but Beatrice was worried about becoming pregnant by Deflores and so she wanted to marry Alsemero quickly.

What Tomazo wanted as fair satisfaction was the blood of the murderer.

Vermandero said:

"His most certain falsehood!"

Vermandero believed that Alonzo had jilted Beatrice, almost leaving her at the altar. Alonzo had then fled.

Alonzo's corpse had not been found, but Tomazo believed that Alonzo had been murdered.

Vermandero continued:

"This is the place, indeed; his breach of faith — his desertion of her — has too much marred and injured both my abused love, the honorable love I reserved for him, and it has too much mocked my daughter's joy.

"The prepared morning — the morning of the intended marriage — blushed at his infidelity; he left contempt and scorn to throw upon those friends whose belief in Alonzo hurt them.

"Oh, it was most ignoble of him to take his flight so unexpectedly and throw such public wrongs on those who loved him!"

"Then this is all your answer?" Tomazo asked.

"It is too fair for one of his alliance — his family — and I warn you that this place will no more see you," Vermandero said. "You are no longer welcome here."

Vermandero exited.

Deflores entered the scene.

Tomazo said:

"The best thing is that there is more ground to meet a man's revenge on."

He meant that he could get revenge here or elsewhere. Or he meant that there was another way to find the information he wanted: the identity of his brother's murderer. Deflores might be able to help him.

He then said:

"Honest Deflores."

"That's my name indeed," Deflores said. "Have you seen the bride? Good sweet sir, which way did she go?"

Tomazo said, "I have blessed — protected — my eyes from seeing such a false one."

He had blessed his eyes by not seeing her. He had avoided Beatrice's evil eye.

Deflores said to himself, "I'd like to get away from here. This man's not for my company. I smell his brother's blood when I come near him."

"Come here, kind and true one," Tomazo said. "I remember that my brother loved thee well."

Deflores replied:

"Oh, he loved me purely and absolutely, dear sir!"

He then said to himself:

"I think that I am now again killing him — Tomazo brings the deed so fresh to my mind."

"Thou can guess, sirrah, that one honest friend has an instinct of feeling suspicion at some foul guilty person," Tomazo said.

Tomazo believed that Deflores was an honest friend to Alonzo, and therefore, he might know or suspect something about Alonzo's murder.

Deflores said:

"Alas, sir, I am so charitable that I think no one is worse than myself.

"You did not see the bride then?"

"I prefer not to name her," Tomazo said. "Isn't she wicked?"

Deflores said:

"No, no, she is a pretty, easy, round-packed sinner —"

"Easy" can mean "of easy virtue." But an easy sinner is a person who commits small sins: sins that cause little discomfort.

"Round-packed" may mean "with feminine curves" or "pleasantly plumb," or it may mean that a round circle of her body is frequently packed with a penis.

Deflores continued:

"— as most ladies are, else you might think I flatter her; but, sir, most ladies are by no means wicked until they are so old that their sins and vices — and chins and noses — meet, and they greet witches."

The sins may be small sins that have grown into great vices of the kind that witches perform.

According to Dante, lust is the least evil of the seven deadly sins. In his *Inferno*, the sins that are punished grow worse the deeper you go. Lust is punished high in the Inferno; the worst sin — treachery against God — is punished at the bottom of the Inferno.

Deflores thinks that most ladies are guilty of lust, and as time continued and they grow older, they become guilty of worse sins.

Deflores continued:

"Someone is calling me, I think, sir."

Deflores then said to himself:

"His company even overlays and oppresses my conscience."

He exited.

Tomazo said to himself:

"That Deflores has a wondrously honest heart. He'll bring it out in time, I'm sure of it."

"Bring it out" means 1) reveal his good heart, or 2) reveal the identity of the murderer of Alonzo.

Alsemero entered the scene. This was his wedding day.

Tomazo said to himself:

"Oh, here's the vainglorious master of the day's joy. It will not be long until he and I reckon and settle our accounts."

He said out loud:

"Sir."

"You are most welcome," Alsemero said.

"You may call that word 'welcome' back," Tomazo said. "I do not think I am welcome, nor do I wish to be."

"It is strange that you found the way to this house then," Alsemero said.

"I wish I'd never known the cause for me to come here," Tomazo said. "I'm not one of those, sir, who come to give you joy and swill your wine. It is a more precious liquor — that is, liquid — that must allay the fiery thirst I bring."

That liquid was blood. Tomazo wanted the blood of the murderer.

"Your words and you appear to me great strangers," Alsemero said.

He had not expected Tomazo to be hostile to him.

Tomazo said:

"Time and our swords may make us more acquainted. This is the reason why: I should have a brother in your place as bridegroom to Beatrice.

"How treachery and malice have disposed of him, I'm bound to enquire of him who holds his right, which never could come fairly."

Tomazo believed that it was possible Alsemero had murdered Alonzo in order to marry Beatrice. Alsemero had gotten both Alonzo's intended bride and intended dowry.

"You must look to answer for that accusation, sir," Alsemero said.

They could fight a duel.

Tomazo said:

"Fear not; I'll have it ready drawn at our next meeting."

"It" referred to his sword, but "it ready drawn" also could mean a legal document drawn up to respond to an accusation.

Tomazo continued:

"Keep your day solemn. Farewell, I will not disturb your wedding. I'll bear the pain with patience for a time."

He exited.

Alsemero said to himself:

"It is somewhat ominous, this: a quarrel entered upon this day — my wedding day.

"My innocence relieves me. I should be wondrously sad otherwise."

Jasperino entered the scene.

Alsemero said:

"Jasperino, I have news to tell thee, strange news."

"I have some news, too, that I think as strange as yours," Jasperino said. "I wish that I might keep my news, provided that my faith and friendship might be kept in it. Indeed, sir, dispense a little with my zeal, and let it cool in this."

Jasperino had news that he did not want to tell Alsemero, but as his friend, he felt that he had to tell him. Indeed, Jasperino would prefer or almost prefer to be a lesser friend to Alsemero if that meant that he did not have to tell Alsemero this news.

"This puts me on and makes me curious and blames thee for thy slowness," Alsemero said.

Alsemero wanted to hear the news.

"All may prove to be nothing," Jasperino said. "It may prove to be only a friendly fear — an over-concern for you — that leapt from me, sir."

"No question it may prove to be nothing," Alsemero said. "Let's partake of it, though. Tell me your news."

Jasperino said:

"It was Diaphanta's chance — for to that wench I pretend honest and honorable love, and she deserves it — to leave me in a back part of the house, a place we chose for private conversation."

The word "pretend" is ambiguous. In addition to its usual meaning, in this society it can mean 1) offer or proffer, or 2) profess.

Jasperino had earlier spoken bawdily to Diaphanta, but she was still a virgin when she very recently talked to Beatrice. It is possible that Jasperino sincerely professed his love to Diaphanta.

Jasperino continued:

"Diaphanta was no sooner gone, but instantly I heard your bride's voice in the next room to me and, lending more attention, I found Deflores louder than she."

"Deflores?" Alsemero said. "Thou are out — mistaken — now."

"You'll tell me more soon," Jasperino said.

Soon, Alsemero would say something different. Or: Soon, Alsemero would be angry and say harsh words.

"Still, I'll forestall thee," Alsemero said. "The very sight of Deflores is poison to Beatrice."

"That made me stagger and hesitate, too, but at her return Diaphanta confirmed it."

Diaphanta knew the sound of Deflores' voice.

"Diaphanta!" Alsemero said.

"Then we both started to listen, and words passed like those that challenge interest in a woman," Jasperino said.

Deflores was claiming his "right" to sleep with Beatrice as if he owned a piece of her.

This conversation that Jasperino and Diaphanta had overheard occurred after Diaphanta's recent talk with Beatrice about taking her place in bed.

"Be quiet," Alsemero said. "Quench thy zeal. It is dangerous to thy bosom."

In other words: Be quiet, or we shall fight a duel.

"Then truth is full of peril," Jasperino said.

Alsemero said:

"Such truths are.

"Oh, if she were the sole glory of the earth, had eyes that could shoot fire into kings' breasts, and were touched and tainted, then she sleeps not here in my bed.

"Yet I have time, although night is near, to be resolved and satisfied whether she is a virgin, and please do not weigh me — judge me — by my outbursts of passion."

"I never judge a friend in that way," Jasperino said.

Alsemero said:

"That is done charitably."

He gave Jasperino a key and said:

"That key will lead thee to an ingenious secret that a Chaldean — an astrologer — taught me; I've made my study into some secrets.

"Bring from my closet a glass vial inscribed there with the letter M, and do not ask me about my purpose."

"It shall be done, sir," Jasperino said.

He exited.

Alsemero said:

"How can this hang together and make sense?"

In other words: How can all this be true?

Alsemero continued:

"Not an hour ago, her serving-woman came pleading her lady's fears, describing her as the timidest virgin who ever shrunk at the name of Man, and so modest that she ordered her serving-woman to weep out her request to me that she might come obscurely — in the dark — to my bosom."

Beatrice entered the scene.

She said to herself, "All things go well. My serving-woman's preparing yonder for her sweet voyage, which I am grieved to lose. Necessity compels it; I lose everything, otherwise."

The "sweet voyage" was sex: a voyage from virginity to sexually experienced.

A woman is the weaker vessel.

A "voyage" can be a pilgrimage.

Alsemero said to himself:

"Ha! Modesty's shrine is set in yonder forehead. I cannot be too sure, though."

He said out loud:

"My Joanna."

"Sir, I was bold to weep a message to you," Beatrice Joanna said. "Pardon my modest fears."

Alsemero said to himself:

"A dove's not meeker than she is. Her reputation has been falsely accused and slandered, without question."

Jasperino entered the scene. He was carrying the vial.

Alsemero said out loud to him:

"Oh, have you come, sir?"

Beatrice said to herself, "The glass vial, upon my life! I see the letter."

"Sir, this is M," Jasperino said.

"It is," Alsemero said.

"I am suspected," Beatrice said to herself.

"How fitly our bride comes to partake with us!" Alsemero said.

"What is it, my lord?" Beatrice asked.

"It is no hurt," Alsemero said.

"Sir, pardon me, I seldom taste of any composition — any mixture," Beatrice said.

Many mixtures were medicinal.

"But this upon my warrant you shall venture on," Alsemero said. "You will taste this mixture. I guarantee that it is safe."

"I fear it will make me ill," Beatrice said.

"Heaven forbid that," Alsemero said.

Beatrice said to herself, "I must rely on my cunning. I know the effects of the liquid. I need to just feign them handsomely and aptly."

Alsemero said quietly to Jasperino, "It has a secret virtue — a secret effect — that will never miss, sir, upon a virgin."

"Treble qualitied," Jasperino whispered back to Alsemero.

He may have recognized the vial or have done some reading while getting the vial. Or he may have already known that the liquid's power was very high.

Beatrice drank the liquid and then she yawned and sneezed.

Alsemero whispered to Jasperino, "By all that's virtuous, it takes effect as intended there — it proceeds!"

Beatrice had exhibited the correct symptoms.

Jasperino whispered back to Alsemero, "This is the strangest trick to know a maiden by."

Beatrice laughed and said: "Ha! Ha! Ha! You have given me joy of heart to drink, my lord."

"No, thou have given me such joy of heart as never can be blasted and blighted," Alsemero said.

"What's the matter, sir?" Beatrice asked.

She pretended to be sad.

Alsemero whispered to Jasperino:

"See, now her mood is settled in a melancholy; it keeps both the time and method."

He then said out loud to Beatrice Joanna:

"My Joanna, you are as chaste as the breath of Heaven or the morning's womb that brings the day forth, and thus my love encloses thee."

He hugged her.

They exited.

Isabella and Lollio talked together in a room in Alibius' house. Isabella was holding a love letter.

Isabella said, "Oh, Heaven! Is this the waiting and waxing Moon? Does love turn fool, run mad, and all at once? Sirrah, here's a madman akin to the fool, too, a lunatic lover."

The fool she meant was Antonio.

A waiting Moon is an ominous Moon. The love letter was not from Isabella's husband.

A waxing Moon is a growing Moon. The Moon was supposed to have an effect on madness. A waxing Moon could make a madman even madder.

The madman who had sent the letter was Franciscus. He and Lollio, a fool, were pursuing Isabella. Another "fool," or fool, Antonio, was also pursuing Isabella.

Fools and madmen pursue married women.

Lollio said, "No, no, not he I brought the letter from."

He had delivered a letter from a madman to her.

"Compare his inside with his outward appearance and tell me," Isabella said.

Isabella had not opened the letter; she had read only the inscription on the outside of the letter. She also wondered about the madman's true intentions.

Lollio, who had also read the outward inscription, said, "The out's mad, I'm sure of that; I had a taste of it."

Franciscus had beaten Lollio.

Lollio read the outside inscription out loud:

"*To the bright Andromeda, chief chambermaid to the Knight of the Sun, at the sign of Scorpio, in the middle region, sent by the bellows-mender of Aeolus. Pay the post.*"

The hero Perseus rescued Andromeda from a dragon.

In Franciscus' inscription, Perseus is Franciscus, Andromeda is Isabella, and the dragon is Alibius (or Lollio).

Chambermaids can be lascivious. Think of Diaphanta.

The Knight of the Sun is the chivalric hero of the romance *The Mirror of Knighthood.*

Scorpio may be the name of an inn where Andromeda and the Knight of the Sun are staying.

Scorpio is the astrological sign that governs the sexual organs, and "middle region" is where those sexual organs are located. (In astrology, "middle region" means the fifth to eighth months of the year.)

Aeolus is the god of the winds. Bellows are used to blow air on a fire to make it hotter. Franciscus would like to sexually heat up Isabella.

The middle regions of the human body produce winds: farts.

The post is the bearer of the letter: Lollio.

Lollio then said:

"This is stark madness."

Isabella said, "Now look at the inside. "

He opened the letter, and she read over his shoulder:

"*Sweet lady, having now cast off this counterfeit cover of a madman, I appear to your best judgment a true and faithful lover of your beauty.*"

Franciscus was saying that he was not mad, just pretending to be mad so he could pursue her.

"He is mad still," Lollio said.

Isabella read out loud:

"*If any fault you find, chide those perfections in you that have made me imperfect; it is the same sun that causes to grow and forces to wither —*"

Isabella's perfections have made Franciscus imperfect: They have tempted him to pursue her.

Lollio interrupted, "Oh, rogue!"

Isabella continued reading out loud:

"*— shapes and transhapes, destroys and builds again. I come in winter to you dismantled — stripped — of my proper ornaments; by the sweet splendor of your cheerful smiles, I spring and live a lover.*"

Franciscus was wearing the clothing of a madman; he was not wearing his own fine clothing.

"He is a mad rascal still," Lollio said.

Isabella continued reading out loud:

"Don't tread underfoot the man who shall appear an honor to your bounties. I remain, mad until I speak with you, from whom I expect my cure, yours all, or one beside himself, Franciscus."

If Isabella is kind and generous to him, he will show himself to be a gentleman.

"Beside himself" means "not himself, because distracted and made mad by love."

"You are likely to have a fine time of it," Lollio said. "My master and I may give up our professions; I am sure that you can cure fools and madmen faster than we, with little pains, too."

She could "cure" Franciscus and Antonio by having sex with them; they would no longer need to retain their disguises.

"Very likely," Isabella said.

Lollio said:

"One thing I must tell you, mistress: You perceive that I know about your skill; if I find you minister once and set the trade, I will put in for my thirds."

If Isabella were to commit adultery and then set up business as a whore, Lollio wanted a third of the profits, and/or a third of the sex. He would share her sexually with her husband and with the man with whom she had committed adultery and with her customers.

But the words also meant that if Isabella were to go into business as a treater of madmen and fools, which was the business of Alibius and Lollio, then Lollio wanted a third of the profits.

Lollio continued:

"I shall be mad or fool else."

Isabella said:

"The first place is thine, believe it, Lollio."

The first place is "mad."

She then said:

"If I do fall —"

She may have wanted to continue with "— but I won't."

Before she could finish her sentence, Lollio said, "I fall upon you."

Isabella said, "So."

This answer can mean, "Ha!" or "It won't happen."

"Well, I stand to my venture," Lollio said.

He would abide by what he said and accept either gain or loss.

"Stand to" can also mean "have an erection."

"But give me thy counsel now," Isabella said. "How shall I deal with the madmen and fools?"

"Why, do you mean to deal with them?" Lollio asked.

"Deal with" can mean "treat," but Lollio preferred the bawdy meaning: "have sex with."

"Nay, I mean the fair understanding — the non-bawdy meaning," Isabella said. "How to use them."

"Use" can mean 1) treat, or 2) have sex with.

"Abuse them," Lollio said. "That's the way to madden the fool and make a fool of the madman, and then you use them kindly — you treat them according to their natures."

One kind of abuse would be for Isabella to disguise herself and deceive Franciscus and Antonio the way that they had disguised themselves and deceived her.

Isabella said:

"It is easy. I'll practice; observe it."

"Practice" can mean "scheme and deceive."

Isabella then said:

"Give me the key to thy wardrobe."

Lollio gave her the key.

"There," he said. "Outfit yourself for them, and I'll fit them both — I'll get them ready — for you."

"Take thou no further notice than the outside," Isabella said.

In other words: 1) Pay attention to what I will be wearing, not to my body under the clothing, 2) Stay here. Don't watch me dress, and 3) When I am in disguise as a madwoman, respond to me as if I were a madwoman.

She exited.

"Not an inch," Lollio said. "I'll put you to the inside."

If Lollio had his preference, his inches would not be outside, but inside, her.

Alibius entered the scene.

"Lollio, are thou there?" Alibius said. "Will all be perfect, do thou think? Tomorrow night, as if to close up the solemnity, Vermandero expects us."

Alibius was thinking about the eccentric dance of the madmen and fools.

"I mistrust — am worried about — the madmen most," Lollio said. "The fools will do well enough: I have taken pains with them."

"Bah, they cannot miss," Alibius said. "The more absurdity, the more the dance will be commended, as long as no rough behaviors frighten the ladies. They are nice things, thou know."

Lollio said, "You need not fear, sir; as long as we are there with our commanding pizzles, they'll be as tame as the ladies themselves."

A "pizzle" is a penis.

Pizzles are whips made from the dried penises of bulls.

"I will see them rehearse once more before they go," Alibius said.

Lollio said:

"I was about to do it, sir.

"Take care of the madmen's morris — their country dance — and let me alone with the fools. There is one or two whose fooling I mistrust; I'll instruct them, and then they shall rehearse the whole measure."

Alibius said:

"Do so. I'll see the music prepared.

"But Lollio, by the way, how does my wife endure her restraint? Doesn't she grudge it? Doesn't she complain?"

Alibius was not allowing his wife to leave the house.

Lollio said:

"So, so. She takes some pleasure in the house; she would be abroad — out of doors — else."

The "pleasure" may be the pursuit of her by Antonio, Franciscus, and Lollio. So says Lollio.

Lollio continued:

"You must allow her a little more length; she's kept too short."

Lollio being Lollio, he was talking about length of penis, as well as length of leash.

"She shall go along to Vermandero's with us," Alibius said. "That will serve her for a month's liberty."

"What's that on your face, sir?" Lollio asked.

"Where, Lollio?" Alibius said. "I see nothing."

"I beg your mercy, sir, it is your nose!" Lollio said. "It looks like the trunk of a young elephant."

Some people such as Lollio wanted to lead Alibius by the nose.

"Bah, rascal," Alibius said. "I'll prepare the music, Lollio."

Alibius exited.

Lollio said:

"Do, sir; and I'll dance the while.

"Tony, where are thou, Tony?"

Antonio entered the scene and said, "Here I am, cousin. Where are thou?"

"Come, Tony, show me the footmanship I taught you," Lollio said.

"I had rather ride, cousin," Antonio said.

He meant a sexual riding.

Lollio said:

"Aye, a whip take you, but I'll keep you out."

If necessary, he would use a whip on Antonio, but he would keep him out of Isabella's vagina.

He continued:

"Vault in — jump into the dance. Look, Tony."

He danced and sang:

"Fa, la la la la."

Antonio danced and sang, "Fa, la la la la."

"There, an honor," Lollio said, bowing.

An honor is a bow with a bended knee. Courtiers would "make a leg": They would make a deep bow with the right leg bent back.

Antonio asked, "Is this an honor, coz?"

He bowed.

"Yes, if it please your worship," Lollio said.

"Does honor bend in the hams, coz?" Antonio asked.

In this society, the "hams" are the hollow parts at the back of the knees.

He was asking about the bow, but the question can mean, "Does honor abase itself?"

A man of higher social class could bow and abase himself to a woman of a lower class so that he could have sex with her.

Lollio replied, "By the Virgin Mary, it does, as low as worship, squireship, nay, yeomanry itself sometimes, from whence it first stiffened. There rise a caper."

Some high-ranking men were addressed with the title "Your Worship."

"Squire" and "yeoman" are names used in two different social classes.

"Stiffened" can mean 1) "grow formal," or 2) "grow an erection."

A caper is a frolic. Sex is supposed to be fun.

A caper is also a leap in a dance.

Honor can abase itself. It can seek liaisons with people of a lower social class.

Antonio was of a higher social class than Isabella.

Antonio asked, "Caper after an honor, coz?"

Hmm.

Caper after an on-her?

Lollio said, "Very proper, for honor is just a caper. It rises as fast and high, has a knee or two, and falls to the ground again. You can remember your figure, Tony?"

In the missionary position, knees are bent.

"Rises" and "falls" are words that can be applied to erections.

"Figure" means 1) bow, 2) appearance, and 3) dance.

Lollio exited.

Antonio said, "Yes, cousin, when I see thy figure, I can remember mine."

Isabella entered the scene, disguised as a madwoman.

Antonio resumed dancing.

Isabella said:

"Hey, how he treads the air! Shoo, shoo, the other way: He burns his wings else. Here's wax enough below, Icarus, more than will be canceled these eighteen Moons."

Icarus was the son of Daedalus, who designed the labyrinth on the island of Crete to house the Minotaur, the half-bull, half-human, man-eating monster. After Daedalus and his son were imprisoned, Daedalus designed wings made of feathers and wax so that he and his son could fly over the sea to freedom. The wings worked, but Icarus flew too close to the Sun, the heat of which melted the wax, causing the feathers to molt. Icarus fell into the sea and drowned. Icarus could have lived, but his exuberance caused his death.

Wax was used to seal legal documents. "Cancelling" can mean "breaking." If Isabella were to commit adultery, she would be breaking her marriage contract. Perhaps she had been married for eighteen months.

Isabella continued:

"He's down! He's down! What a terrible fall he had!

"Stand up, thou son of Cretan Daedalus, and let us tread the lower labyrinth. I'll bring thee to the clue."

In mythology, Ariadne gave Theseus, who killed the Minotaur, the clue — the ball of twine — that he unrolled and used to find his way out of the labyrinth that Daedalus constructed.

"Tread" can mean 1) dance, and 2) have sex.

"The lower labyrinth" can figuratively mean a woman's sex organs.

Possibly, Alibius is the figurative Minotaur.

Not recognizing her, Antonio said, "Please, coz, let me alone."

Disguised as a madwoman, Isabella said:

"Aren't thou drowned? About thy head I saw a heap of clouds wrapped like a Turkish turban on thy back, a crooked chameleon-color rainbow hung like a tiara down to thy hams."

She pretended to be surprised that he had not drowned, as Icarus had in the myth.

A tiara is a headdress or turban with a long tail.

Disguised as a madwoman, Isabella then said:

"Let me suck out those billows in thy belly."

If he had been in the sea, he would have swallowed a lot of water and had billows of it in his stomach.

A billow is a great swelling wave.

In this society, an alternate spelling of "billow" was "bellow."

According to the *Oxford English Dictionary*, one definition of "Bellows" is "*figurative*. Applied to that which blows up or fans the fire of passion, discord, etc."

A penis can fan the fire of passion. Certainly, the production of semen involves fanning the fire of passion.

If semen can be likened to water, then ...

Hmm.

The author of this retelling is shocked. Really. I am.

Disguised as a madwoman, Isabella continued:

"Listen to how they roar and rumble in the straits! May God bless and protect thee from the pirates."

Figuratively, the straits are intestines.

Literal straits often harbored pirates.

Disguised as a madwoman, Isabella attempted to kiss him.

Antonio said, "A pox upon you! Let me alone!"

He was cursing her.

Disguised as a madwoman, Isabella said:

"Why should thou mount as high as Mercury unless thou had the reversion of his place?"

Mercury was the messenger of the gods. Like the other gods, he often had affairs with mortals. Such affairs involve mounting.

"Reversion of his place" means the right of succession to his office.

Disguised as a madwoman, Isabella continued:

"Stay in the Moon with me, Endymion, and we will rule these wild rebellious waves that would have drowned my love."

Endymion was a handsome youth whom the Moon loved.

The Moon controls the tides.

Still not recognizing Isabella, Antonio said, "I'll kick thee if thou touch me again, thou wild unshapen antic. I am no fool, you bedlam!"

An "unshapen antic" is a deformed, grotesque figure.

Disguised as a madwoman, Isabella said, "But you are, as surely as I am, mad. Have I put on this habit — this clothing — of a frantic madwoman with love as full of fury to beguile the nimble eye of watchful jealousy, and am I thus rewarded?"

Recognizing her, Antonio said, "Ha, dearest beauty!"

Isabella said:

"No, I have no beauty now, nor have I ever had, except what was in my garments."

In other words, Antonio had fallen in love with her clothing, not with her.

She continued:

"You are a quick-sighted lover? Don't come near me! Keep your caparisons; you are aptly clad."

"Caparisons" are used to cover a horse.

She continued:

"I came a feigner to return stark mad."

Isabella was saying that she had come here pretending that she was insane, but she was leaving as someone who was truly mad.

Isabella was also telling Antonio to keep wearing his fool's clothing because it suited him.

Isabella exited.

Lollio entered as Antonio called after her, "Stay, or I shall change condition and become as you are."

In other words: If she left him, he would truly become mad.

He acted as if he would run after her.

"Why, Tony, where do you think you're going now?" Lollio said. "Why, fool!"

"Whose fool, usher of idiots?" Antonio said. "You coxcomb! I have fooled too much."

An usher is 1) a door-keeper, and/or 2) an assistant teacher.

"It would be best for you to be mad for another while then," Lollio said.

"So I am," Antonio said. "I am stark mad; I have cause enough. And I could throw the full effects on thee and beat thee like a Fury."

Furies were avenging spirits from the Land of the Dead.

Lollio said:

"Do not! Do not! I shall not forbear the gentleman under the fool, if you do."

In other words, if you beat me, I will resist even though you are a gentleman under your disguise as a fool.

Lollio then said:

"Alas, I saw through your fox-skin — your disguise — before now.

"Come, I can give you comfort: My mistress loves you, and there is as arrant a madman in the house as you are a fool, your rival, whom she does not love. If after the masque, we can rid her of him, you will earn her love, she says, and the fool shall ride her."

Which fool? Is Lollio, a fool, trying to trick Antonio, a fool?

The riding would be sexual.

"May I believe thee?" Antonio asked.

"Yes, or you may choose whether you will or not," Lollio said.

"She will be eased of him," Antonio said. "I have a good reason for relieving her."

"Well, keep your old station — old position — as a fool for a while longer, and be quiet," Lollio said.

"Tell her I will deserve her love," Antonio said.

"And you are likely to have your desire," Lollio said.

Antonio exited.

Franciscus entered the scene.

He said, "Down, down, down a-down a-down, and then with a horse-trick to kick Latona's forehead and break her bowstring."

The verb "down" can mean to knock a person down.

A horse-trick is 1) horse-play, or 2) a kind of leap.

"A horse-trick" may also mean "a whore's trick."

"Latona" is the Roman name of Leto, the mother of the archer-god Apollo and of Diana, goddess of the hunt. Diana used a bow and arrows while hunting. Franciscus has confused Latona and Diana.

By "Latona," Franciscus meant Isabella. He wanted to break her marriage vows.

Lollio said:

"This is the other counterfeit. I'll put him out of his humor."

He read out loud:

"*Sweet lady, having now cast off this counterfeit cover of a madman, I appear to your best judgment a true and faithful lover of your beauty.*"

He then said:

"This is pretty good for a madman."

"Ha!" Franciscus said. "What's that?"

Lollio read out loud:

"*Chide those perfections in you that made me imperfect.*"

"I am discovered — revealed — to the fool," Franciscus said. "He knows that I am faking my madness."

By "fool," he meant Lollio.

Lollio said to himself:

"I hope to discover — reveal — the fool in you before I have done with you."

He read out loud:

"*Yours all, or one beside himself, Franciscus.*"

He said to himself:

"This madman will mend surely."

In other words: Franciscus will stop pretending to be mad.

"What are you reading, sirrah?" Franciscus asked.

"Your destiny, sir," Lollio said. "You'll be hanged for this trick and another trick that I know."

One trick is the fraud of pretending to be a madman, and the other trick is attempting to commit adultery with Isabella.

"Are thou of counsel with thy mistress?" Franciscus asked. "Are you in her confidence?"

"I am next to her apron strings," Lollio said.

"Give me thy hand," Franciscus said.

Lollio said:

"Wait, let me put yours in my pocket first."

He put the letter in Franciscus' handwriting in his pocket.

In this society, one meaning of "hand" is "handwriting."

Lollio continued:

"Your hand is true, isn't it? It is honest? Will it pick my pocket? I partly fear it because I think it does lie."

"Not in a syllable," Franciscus said.

"So, if you love my mistress as well as you have handled the matter here in this letter, you are likely to be cured of your madness," Lollio said.

"And no one but she can cure it," Franciscus said.

She could "cure" him by having sex with him.

"Well, I'll give you over to her care then, and she shall cast your water next," Lollio said.

Physicians examined a patient's urine in an attempt to determine their health.

One meaning of "cast," according to the *Oxford English Dictionary*, is "to throw" — that is, "to project (anything) with a force of the nature of a jerk, from the hand [...]."

If semen can be likened to water, then ...

Hmm.

Franciscus gave him money and said, "Take this for thy past pains."

"I shall deserve more, sir, I hope," Lollio said. "My mistress loves you, but she must have some proof of your love to her."

"There I meet my wishes," Franciscus said.

That is something he wanted to do.

"That will not serve," Lollio said. "You must meet her enemy and yours."

Meet? As in a duel?

"He's dead already," Franciscus said.

He meant "as good as dead."

"Will you tell me that, and I parted just now from him?" Lollio asked, deliberately misunderstanding him.

"Show me the man," Franciscus said.

Lollio said:

"Aye, that's a right course now: See him before you kill him, in any case; and yet it need not go as far as murder either.

"It is just a fool who haunts the house and my mistress in the disguise of an idiot. Just bang his fools' coat well-favoredly — soundly — and it is well."

"Soundly, soundly," Franciscus said.

"Soundly" means 1) your advice is sound, and 2) he will be soundly beaten.

Lollio said:

"Just spare him until the masque is past; and if you don't find him now in the dance yourself, I'll show you who he is."

Seeing Alibius coming, Lollio said:

"Go in! Go in! My master!"

Alibius entered the scene.

Dancing, Franciscus said, "He handles himself like a feather. Hey!"

Franciscus exited.

"Well done!" Alibius said. "Is everything ready, Lollio?"

"Yes, sir," Lollio said.

Alibius said:

"Go then, and guide them in, Lollio. Entreat your mistress to see this sight."

Lollio exited.

Alibius said loudly to Lollio:

"Listen, isn't there one incurable fool who might be begged? I have friends."

A person might ask in court to become the guardian of a fool. As guardian, he could enjoy the wealth of the fool.

Alibius' friends could be lawyers or people with influence in the judicial system, or they could be people he would like to benefit financially.

"I have him for you, one who shall deserve it, too," Lollio said from another room.

Which one?

Antonio is a fool, but the pretended madman Francisco is also a fool. Lollio, and Alibius himself, are fools.

Alibius said:

"Good boy, Lollio."

Isabella, no longer dressed as a madwoman, entered the scene, followed by Lollio, who brought out the madmen and fools, who danced without music.

Alibius said:

"It is perfect.

"Well, once I prepare the strains of music for their dancing, we shall have coin and credit — money and reputation — for our pains."

CHAPTER 5

— 5.1 —

Alone, Beatrice paced in a room in the castle.

She said to herself:

"A clock struck one, and yet she lies in bed at this time.

"Oh, my fears! This strumpet serves her own ends — it is apparent now. She devours the sexual pleasure with a greedy appetite, and she never minds my honor — my reputation for chastity — or my peace of mind. She makes havoc of my right, but she will pay dearly for it: no trusting her alive with such a secret — I will not trust a person who cannot rule her blood — her sexual passion — to keep her promise."

Beatrice thought that Diaphanta was still having sex with Alsemero.

Beatrice continued saying to herself:

"Besides, I have some suspicion of her faith to me because I was suspected by my lord, and it must come from her."

A clock struck two.

Beatrice continued saying to herself:

"Hark, by my horrors, another clock strikes two."

Deflores entered the scene and said: "Psst, where are you?"

"Deflores?" Beatrice asked.

"Aye," Deflores said. "Hasn't she come from him yet?"

"As I am a living soul, she has not," Beatrice said.

Deflores said, "Surely the devil has sowed his sexual itch inside her. Who'd trust a waiting-woman?"

"I must trust somebody," Beatrice said.

Deflores said:

"Bah, waiting-women are termagants."

A termagant is a bad-tempered woman.

Deflores continued:

"Especially when they fall upon and 'attack' their masters in bed and have their ladies' first fruits, they are mad whelps. You cannot stave them off from game royal then."

The "first fruits" were wedding-night sex.

Staves were used to control animals at bear-baitings.

"Game royal" is game reserved for royals to hunt. The dogs are so eager to hunt that they cannot be stopped from hunting game that is reserved for the royal family to hunt.

Deflores continued:

"You are so harsh and hardy that you ask for no counsel — no advice — from me. And I could have helped you to an apothecary's daughter who would have fallen off and stopped having sex before eleven, and thanked you, too."

Beatrice had come up with the scheme involving Diaphanta without first consulting Deflores.

"Oh, me! Isn't she finished yet?" Beatrice said about Diaphanta. "This whore forgets herself."

Deflores said about Alsemero:

"The rascal fares so well."

Alsemero was enjoying lots of sex.

Alsemero and Diaphanta may have fallen asleep, something that did not occur to Beatrice and Deflores.

Deflores then said:

"Look, you are undone: You are ruined. I see the day-star, I swear by this hand. See Phosphorus plain yonder."

"Phosphorus" is the morning star: Venus.

Another name for the morning star is "Lucifer."

Beatrice said, "Advise me now to fall upon some ruin. There is no safe counsel other than that."

Her first sentence may mean that the best thing for her to do now would be to commit suicide. Or the sentence could mean that she wanted to cause some kind of destruction out of despair.

Deflores said, "Peace, I have it now. For we must force a rising; there's no remedy — no alternative."

Deflores meant that they could cause a disturbance that would make everyone get out of bed. He will explain why.

"How?" Beatrice said. "Take heed of that."

"Tush, be quiet or else give all up," Deflores said.

"Please, I have finished then," Beatrice said.

"This is my plan," Deflores said. "I'll set some part of Diaphanta's bedchamber on fire."

"What!" Beatrice said. "Fire, sir? That may endanger the whole house."

"You talk of danger when your reputation is on fire?" Deflores said

"That's true," Beatrice said. "Do what thou will now."

Deflores said:

"Phooey, I aim at a very rich and successful outcome that strikes all dead sure."

The plan would meet all objectives for sure.

Deflores continued:

"The chimney being on fire, and also only some light parcels in Diaphanta's chamber of the least danger of causing a major fire, if Diaphanta should be met by chance then far from her lodging, which would now be regarded as suspicious, it would be thought that her fears and fright then drove her to seek succor. And if she is not seen or met at all, as is the likeliest to happen, for her own shame she'll hasten towards her lodging. I will be ready with a highly charged gun, as if it were to cleanse the chimney — there, it is a proper plan now — but she shall be the target."

Shooting a gun up a chimney causes soot to fall, thus cleaning the chimney. A chimney must be clean to draw smoke upward.

Creosote, a highly flammable substance, builds up in chimneys and can ignite. Firing a gun up the chimney can clean out the creosote.

Possibly, firing a shotgun up a chimney could put out a small fire.

"I'm forced to love thee now because thou provide so carefully for my honor: my reputation for chastity," Beatrice said.

"By God's eyelid, it concerns the safety of us both and our pleasure and continuance," Deflores said.

If they avoided scandal, they could continue to have an affair. Also, they could continue to live.

"One word now, please," Beatrice said. "What about the servants?"

Deflores said:

"I'll dispatch them, some one way, some another, in the hurry for buckets, hooks, ladders. Don't be afraid."

By "dispatch," Deflores meant that he would give them orders, not kill them.

Deflores continued:

"The deed — Diaphanta's murder — shall find its time, and I've thought since upon a safe conveyance for — a safe way to remove — the body, too. How this fire purifies wit and stimulates my inventiveness! Watch your minute: Act at the proper time."

"Fear keeps my soul upon it," Beatrice said. "I cannot stray from thinking about the right time to act."

Alonzo's ghost entered the scene.

Deflores said:

"Ha! What are thou that takes away the light between that star and me? I don't dread thee!"

A few moments passed, and Deflores said:

"It was just a mist of conscience. All's clear again."

Deflores exited.

Beatrice said:

"Who's that, Deflores? Bless me! It slides by."

Alonzo's ghost exited.

Beatrice continued:

"Some ill thing haunts the house. It has left behind a shivering sweat upon me: I'm afraid now. This night has been so tedious and long and vexatious.

"Oh, this strumpet! Even if she had a thousand lives, he should not leave her until he had destroyed the last."

This was ambiguous:

1) Who is "he"?

2) What does "destroyed" mean?

In the slang of the time, "to die" meant "to have an orgasm."

One meaning: Even if she had a thousand lives, Alsemero would give Diaphanta a thousand orgasms.

Another meaning: Even if she had a thousand lives, Deflores would murder Diaphanta a thousand times.

A clock struck three.

Beatrice continued:

"Listen! Oh, my terrors! Three o'clock struck by the clock at St. Sebastian's Church!"

From inside came shouts: "Fire! Fire! Fire!"

Beatrice said, "Already! How splendid is that man's speed! How heartily and faithfully he serves me! His face makes one loathe him, but if you look upon the care he takes of me, who would not love him? The east is not more beauteous than his service."

The rising sun is beautiful, but also of much value are the light and heat it provides.

"His service" can mean "Deflores' sexual service."

Beatrice may be enjoying the sex she has with Deflores.

From inside came shouts: "Fire! Fire! Fire!"

Deflores entered the scene. Servants ran around. A bell rang.

Deflores said to the servants:

"Away, dispatch — hurry! Hooks, buckets, ladders; that's well done!"

The servants exited.

Deflores then said to Beatrice:

"The fire bell rings. The chimney is fulfilling its responsibility, being on fire. I must carry out my responsibility: The charge — gunpowder — is loaded in the gun, and so the gun is ready."

He exited.

"Here's a man worth loving!" Beatrice said. "Oh, you are a jewel!"

Diaphanta entered the scene.

She said, "Pardon frailty, madam; indeed, I was so well that I completely forgot myself."

Diaphanta had enjoyed — really enjoyed — the sexual experience.

"You have made trim work," Beatrice said.

"Trim" can mean "good" and "neat."

Both "trim" and "work" can mean "have sex."

"What?" Diaphanta asked.

"Hurry quickly to your chamber," Beatrice said. "Your reward follows you."

By "reward," Diaphanta thought that Beatrice meant the thousand ducats.

By "reward," Beatrice meant Diaphanta's death.

"I never made so sweet a bargain," Diaphanta said.

She exited.

Alsemero entered the scene.

"Oh, my dear Joanna!" Alsemero said to Beatrice Joanna. "Alas, have thou risen, too? I was coming, my absolute treasure."

From his words, Beatrice understood that Alsemero had arisen from bed before Diaphanta had.

"When I missed you, I could not choose but follow," Beatrice said.

"Thou are all sweetness," Alsemero said. "The fire is not so dangerous."

"Do you think so, sir?" Beatrice asked.

"Please don't tremble," Alsemero said. "Believe me, the fire is not dangerous."

Vermandero and Jasperino entered the scene.

"Oh, bless my house and me!" Vermandero said.

"My lord your father," Alsemero said to Beatrice.

Deflores entered the scene, carrying a gun.

"Knave, where are you taking that gun?" Vermandero asked.

"To scour the chimney," Deflores said.

He exited.

"Oh, well done, well done," Vermandero said. "That fellow's good on all occasions."

"A wondrously necessary man, my lord," Beatrice said. "Entirely indispensable."

Vermandero said:

"He has a ready wit; he's worth all of them, sir.

"Dog at a house on fire! I have seen him singed before now."

"Dog at a house on fire!" means "He is dogged at harassing and putting out fires."

The gun went off.

Vermandero said:

"Ha! There he goes!"

"It is done," Beatrice said.

"Come, sweet, let's go to bed now," Alsemero said to Beatrice. "Thou will get cold."

"Alas, the fear keeps cold out," Beatrice said. "My heart will find no quiet until I hear how Diaphanta, my poor serving-woman, is. It is her chamber, sir, her lodging chamber, that was on fire."

"How would a fire start there?" Vermandero asked.

"Diaphanta is as good a soul as ever a lady employed, but in her bed-chamber she is negligent and clumsy," Beatrice said. "She escaped a mine twice."

In warfare, a mine was an underground tunnel dug under a fortification so that explosives could be placed in it to destroy the fortification.

Figuratively, a mine is a dangerous situation.

The two times Diaphanta escaped a mine may be when 1) she passed the virginity test, and 2) when she slept with Alsemero without being detected.

A third mine could be Beatrice's anger at Diaphanta's spending so much time in bed with Alsemero.

"Twice?" Vermandero asked.

"Miraculously, twice, sir," Beatrice said.

"Those sleepy sluts are dangerous in a house, even if they are very good as servants," Vermandero said.

The phrase "sleepy slut" meant "lazy, slovenly woman."

The "mines" Vermandero was thinking about may have involved carelessness with candles or fireplaces.

Deflores entered the scene, carrying the burnt corpse of Diaphanta. Burning the corpse helped hide the gunshot wound.

"Oh, poor virginity!" Deflores said. "Thou have paid dearly for it."

Diaphanta had given up her virginity; her reward was her death.

"Bless us!" Vermandero said. "What's that?"

"A thing you all knew once," Deflores said. "Diaphanta's burnt."

"My serving-woman," Beatrice said. "Oh, my serving-woman!"

"Now the flames are greedy for her," Deflores said. "Burnt, burnt, burnt to death, sir."

"Oh, my presaging — my prophetic — soul!" Beatrice said.

"Not a tear more, I charge you by the last embrace I gave you in bed before this raised us out of bed," Alsemero said.

"Now you tie and constrain me," Beatrice said. "Even if she were my sister who died, now she gets no more tears."

A servant entered the scene.

"How are things now?" Vermandero asked.

The servant replied:

"All danger's past; you may now take your rests, my lords. The fire is thoroughly quenched.

"Ah, poor gentlewoman, how soon was she stifled!"

"Stifled" means suffocated. Most fire victims suffocate from lack of oxygen, which is used up feeding the fire. Some fire victims are then burnt.

"Deflores, inter what is left of her, and we as mourners all will follow her," Beatrice said. "I will entreat that honor to my servant, even of my lord and husband himself."

"Command it, sweetness," Alsemero said.

"Which of you spied the fire first?" Beatrice asked.

"It was I, madam," Deflores said.

"And took such pains in it, too?" Beatrice said. "A double goodness! It would be well if he were rewarded."

Deflores had taken pains to set the fire and to put it out.

"He shall be," Vermandero said. "Deflores, call upon me."

"And upon me, sir," Alsemero said.

Deflores would call on them to get a reward.

Everyone except Deflores exited.

He said to himself:

"Rewarded? By God's precious body, here's a trick beyond me!

"I see in all bouts both of sport and wit ..."

A "bout" is a competition.

"Sport" can mean 1) an entertainment such as fencing, and 2) sex.

Deflores concluded:

"Always a woman strives for the last hit."

The sport of fencing has "hits."

Beatrice was figuratively hitting or striking Vermandero and Alsemero.

Beatrice had succeeded in getting Deflores a reward from Vermandero and Alsemero.

Deflores had murdered Vermandero's prospective son-in-law, and he had cuckolded Alsemero.

Deflores exited.

Alone in a room in the palace, Tomazo said to himself:

"I cannot taste the benefits of life with the same relish that I was accustomed to do.

"I grow weary of Mankind, and I regard Mankind's fellowship as a treacherous, bloody friendship, and because I am ignorant on whom my wrath should settle, I must think that all men are villains; and the next man I meet, whoever he is, I must think that he is the murderer of my most worthy brother."

Deflores walked onto the scene, but then he walked away.

Tomazo continued saying to himself:

"Ha! Who's he? Oh, the fellow whom some call honest Deflores.

"But I think that honesty was hard put to it to come there for a lodging, as if a queen should make her palace out of a pest-house: a hospital for plague patients."

Deflores suffered from a skin condition.

Tomazo's feelings toward Deflores had changed. Previously, in 4.2, he had said to Deflores, "Come here, kind and true one. I remember that my brother loved thee well."

Tomazo continued saying to himself:

"I find a contrariety in nature between that face and me: I have an instinctive hatred for that face. The least occasion would give me game upon him — would incite me to attack him.

"Yet he's so foul one would scarcely touch him with a sword one loved and valued. Deflores is so most deadly venomous that he would go near to poison any weapon that should draw blood on him; one who strikes him with that sword must resolve never to use that sword again in a fight, according to the protocol of honest manly behavior. Some river must devour it; it would not be fit that any man should find it."

After striking Deflores with a sword, Tomazo would throw the sword in a river as it would be unfit for him or any other honest man to use.

Deflores entered the scene again.

Tomazo continued saying to himself:

"What, again! He walks on purpose by me, surely, to choke me with the loathing of his presence, to infect my blood."

"My worthy noble lord," Deflores said.

"Do thou attempt to come near me and breathe upon me?" Tomazo said.

He struck Deflores.

"A blow," Deflores said, drawing his sword.

"Yes, are you so prepared?" Tomazo said. "I'll rather die by the sword like a soldier than die by thy poison like a politician — like a Machiavellian schemer."

Tomazo drew his sword.

"Wait, my lord, as you are honorable," Deflores said.

"All slaves who kill by poison are always cowards," Tomazo said.

Deflores would not fight; therefore, he must be a coward. According to Tomazo, Deflores also used poison to kill people.

Deflores said to himself:

"I cannot strike. I see his brother's wounds freshly bleeding in his eye, as in a crystal ball."

He said out loud:

"I will not question this; I know you are noble. I take my injury with thanks given, sir, like a wise lawyer, and as a favor, I will wear it and tolerate it because of the worthy hand that gave it."

He sheathed his sword.

Deflores said to himself:

"Why did I receive this blow from him who yesterday appeared so strangely loving to me? Oh, but instinct is of a subtler strain; guilt must not walk so near his — Tomazo's — lodge again. He came close to discovering my guilt just now."

In other words: Instinct had made Tomazo suspect that Deflores had killed his brother.

Deflores exited.

Tomazo sheathed his sword and said to himself, "I renounce forever all league and alliance with Mankind until I find this murderer. I'll lock up and suppress even common courtesy, for in the state of ignorance that I live in, a brother may greet his brother's murderer and may wish good speed and success to the villain in a greeting."

Vermandero, Alibius, and Isabella entered the scene.

"Noble Piracquo," Vermandero said.

Tomazo de Piracquo replied, "Please keep on your way, sir. I've nothing to say to you."

"May comforts bless you, sir," Vermandero said.

"I have forsworn and renounced compliment and courtesy; in truth, I have, sir," Tomazo said. "As you are merely a man, I have not left a good wish for you, nor for any man here."

"Unless you are so far in love with grief that you will not part from it upon any terms, we bring news that will make a welcome for us," Vermandero said.

"What news can that be?" Tomazo said, smiling contemptuously.

"Throw no scornful smile upon the good that I bring you and the zeal that I brought to bear to help you, for it is worth more, sir," Vermandero said. "I will not hide from the law or from your just vengeance two of the chiefest men I kept about me."

"Vengeance" meant "private justice." Tomazo could seek out and kill the two men.

"Ha!" Tomazo said.

He realized that Vermandero must be referring to two men who had murdered his — Tomazo's — brother.

Vermandero said, "To give your peace of mind more ample satisfaction, thank these discoverers."

The discoverers were Alibius and Isabella. They had discovered something secret and had told Vermandero.

"If you bring that calm, name but the manner I shall ask forgiveness in for that scornful, contemptuous smile I made upon you," Tomazo said. "Tell me what I need to do to earn your forgiveness. I'll perfect it with reverence that belongs to a sacred altar."

He knelt.

Vermandero raised him and said:

"Good sir, rise. Why, now you over-do as much at this hand as you fell short at the other."

Before, Tomazo had been too angry at him. Now, Tomazo was too apologetic to him.

Vermandero said:

"Speak, Alibius."

Alibius said:

"It was my wife's fortune, as she is most lucky at a discovery to find out recently within our hospital of fools and madmen two counterfeits who had slipped into these disguises."

He meant the disguises of madman and of fool.

He may have been holding the disguises of the false madman and the false fool.

Alibius continued:

"Their names are Franciscus and Antonio."

"Both are my men, sir, and I ask no favor — no lenient treatment — for them," Vermandero said.

Alibius said, "Now for that which draws suspicion to their disguising clothing of madman and fool: The time of their disguisings agrees exactly with the day of the murder."

"Oh, blest revelation!" Tomazo said.

Vermandero said, "Nay, there is more; there is more, sir. I'll not spare my own men in the way of justice. They both feigned a journey to Briamata, and so obtained permission to leave. My love and respect for them was much abused in it."

Vandermero has made a mistake. Actually, one of the men was supposed to be going to Valencia.

Tomazo said:

"Time's too precious to be wasted now; you have brought a peace that the riches of five kingdoms could not purchase. Be my most happy guide to them.

"I thirst for them. Like subtle lightning I will wind about them and melt their marrow inside them."

Some people in this society believed that lightning killed by melting marrow without breaking the skin.

They exited.

Alsemero and Jasperino talked together in Alsemero's chamber.

Jasperino said, "Your confidence in my allegations against Beatrice, I'm sure, is now of proof: Your confidence is now as strong as armor. The prospect from the garden has showed enough for deep suspicion."

Previously, Jasperino had told Alsemero that there was evidence that Beatrice was unfaithful to him. Alsemero's confidence in Jasperino had been lacking then, but now Alsemero himself had evidence that backed up Jasperino's suspicion. Together, they had seen Beatrice and Deflores together in the garden.

Alsemero said, "The black mask of Beatrice's hypocrisy that so continually was worn upon her face condemns her true face as ugly before it is seen, and it condemns her seeming despite to him, which was so seemingly bottomless."

The black mask was Beatrice's seeming hatred of Deflores, but her true face was her sexual relationship with Deflores.

Jasperino said:

"Touch it home then, and get to the bottom of it. Probe this corrupt relationship. It is not a shallow probe that can search this ulcer soundly. I fear you'll find it full of corruption."

Wounds would be probed to see how deep they were. The metaphorical wound of Alsemero's and Beatrice's relationship was deep.

Jasperino continued:

"It is fit that I leave you. She meets you opportunely from that walk. She took the back door at his parting with her."

Jasperino exited.

Alsemero asked himself:

"Did my fate wait for this unhappy stroke at my first sight of woman?"

Beatrice was the first woman with whom he fell in love.

Beatrice entered the scene.

Alsemero said to himself:

"She's here."

"Alsemero!" Beatrice said.

"How are you?" Alsemero asked.

"How am I?" Beatrice said. "Alas! How are you? You don't look well."

"You read me well enough," Alsemero said. "I am not well."

"Not well, sir?" Beatrice said. "Is it in my power to better you?"

"Yes," Alsemero said.

"Then you are cured again," Beatrice said.

"Please answer one question for me, lady," Alsemero said.

"If I can," Beatrice said.

"None can so surely answer it," Alsemero said. "Are you honest? Are you chaste?"

"Ha! Ha! Ha! That's a broad question, my lord," Beatrice said.

"But that's not a modest — a chaste — answer, my lady," Alsemero said. "Do you laugh? My fears are strong upon me."

Beatrice replied, "It is innocence that smiles, and no rough brow — frowning forehead — can take away the dimple in her cheek. Suppose I should strain a tear that would fill the vault of Heaven, which — smiling or crying — would you give the better faith to?"

Alsemero said:

"It would be only hypocrisy of a sadder, more serious, darker color, but the same cloth.

"Neither your smiles nor your tears shall move or flatter me from my belief: You are a whore."

"What a horrid sound that word has!" Beatrice said. "It blasts a beauty into a deformity. Upon whatsoever face that breath falls, it strikes it and makes it ugly. Oh, you have ruined what you can never repair again!"

"I'll demolish all and seek out truth within you, if there is any left," Alsemero said. "Let your sweet tongue forestall my rifling of your heart by telling the truth; there in your heart, I'll ransack and tear out my suspicion."

"You may, sir. It is an easy passage to my heart," Beatrice said, "yet if you please, show me the ground and basis whereon you lost your love. My spotless virtue can only tread on it — crush it — before I perish."

The verb "tread" can also mean "have sex."

Alsemero said:

"The ground and basis of my belief that you are unchaste is unanswerable. You cannot refute it.

"It is a ground you cannot stand on. You fall down beneath all grace and goodness when you set your ticklish — your lascivious — heel on it. There was a visor — a black mask — over that cunning face, and that became you. Now impudence and shamelessness rides upon your face in triumph. How comes this tender reconcilement else between you and your despite — the man you pretend to despise — your rancorous loathing, Deflores?

"He whom your eye was sore at sight of, he's now become your arms' supporter, your lips' saint."

"Is there the cause?" Beatrice said.

"Oh, there is worse: your lust's devil, your adultery with him," Alsemero said.

"If anyone but yourself would say that, it would turn him into a villain," Beatrice said.

"It was witnessed by the counsel of your bosom: Diaphanta," Alsemero said.

"Is your witness dead then?" Beatrice asked.

"It is to be feared that death was the wages of her knowledge, poor soul," Alsemero said. "She lived not long after the discovery."

"Then hear a story of not much less horror than this your false suspicion is beguiled with," Beatrice said. "To your bed's scandal I stand up and plead innocence, which even the guilt of one black other deed will stand for proof of: My love for you has made me a cruel murderess."

The scandal of Alsemero's bed was that he had committed adultery in it: He had had sex with Diaphanta in it.

Beatrice is innocent of adultery because she has never had sex with Alsemero and therefore cannot have been unfaithful to him. Since her marriage to Alsemero, she has not had sex with anyone.

When she and Deflores met in the garden, they had only talked. They said enough for Alsemero to be certain that Beatrice and Deflores were sleeping together.

But she has been an accessory to murder — two murders — because she loved Alsemero.

"Ha!" Alsemero said.

Beatrice said, "I have been a bloody murderer. I have kissed poison for it. I have stroked a serpent, that thing of hate, worthy in my esteem of no better employment, and him who is most worthy to be so employed I caused to murder that innocent Alonzo de Piracquo, having no better means than that worst, to assure yourself to me."

In order to have Alsemero as her husband, she had used Deflores to murder Alonzo, and then she had been forced to kiss poison and stroke a serpent: to have sex with Deflores.

She had sexually stroked Deflores' "serpent."

Alsemero said:

"Oh, the place itself ever since has been crying for vengeance, the temple where blood and beauty — Deflores and you, Beatrice — first unlawfully fired their devotion and quenched the life of the right one."

The place and the temple are each the murdered body of Alonzo, who is "the right one": the one who should have married Beatrice.

1 Corinthians 9:19 states, *"What? know ye not that your body is the temple of the Holy Ghost which is in you, which ye have of God, and ye are not your own?"* (King James Version).

Alternatively, "blood and beauty" are "sexual passion and beauty." The temple is a physical church, and "the right one" is "devotion to God."

Alsemero continued:

"Suspicion was in my fears at first: suspicion will have its due vengeance now. Oh, thou are all deformed!"

"Don't forget, sir, it was done for your sake," Beatrice said. "Shall greater dangers make the less welcome?"

Beatrice had dared much to marry Alsemero. Should that daring make him welcome her less?

"Oh, thou should have gone a thousand leagues out of your way to have avoided this dangerous bridge between us, which you built out of blood," Alsemero said. "Here we are lost."

"Remember that I am true to your bed," Beatrice said.

Since her marriage to Alsemero, she has not had sex with Deflores — there hasn't been time and opportunity.

Jasperino and Alsemero had seen Beatrice and Deflores talking in the garden; they did not see them having sex.

Alsemero said:

"The bed itself is a charnel-house, a place for dead bodies. The sheets are shrouds for murdered carcasses.

"I must ask for a pause to consider what I must do in this.

"In the meantime, you shall only be my prisoner. Enter my private room."

Beatrice exited.

Alsemero said to himself:

"I'll be your keeper for the time being. Oh, in what part of this sad story shall I first begin?"

Deflores entered the scene.

Alsemero said to himself:

"Ha! This same fellow has given me a place to begin: with him."

He said out loud:

"Deflores."

"Noble Alsemero!" Deflores said.

"I can tell you news, sir," Alsemero said. "My wife has commended her to you."

Alsemero meant that Beatrice had sent her greetings to him.

"That's news indeed, my lord," Deflores said. 'I think she would commend me to the gallows if she could — she always loved me so 'well.' I thank her."

"What's this blood upon your collar, Deflores?" Alsemero asked.

"Blood? No, surely it has been washed since," Deflores said.

"Since when, man?" Alsemero asked.

"Since the other day I got a knock in a sword-and-dagger school," Deflores said. "I think the blood has been washed out."

Alsemero said:

"Yes, it is almost out, but it is perceived, though."

Murder will out.

Alsemero continued:

"I had forgotten my message; this it is: What is the going price for murder?"

"What, sir?" Deflores asked.

"I ask you, sir," Alsemero said. "My wife's indebted to you, she tells me, for a brave, bloody blow you gave for her sake upon Alonzo de Piracquo."

"Upon him?" Deflores said. "It was quite through him, surely. Has she confessed it?"

"As surely as death to both of you, and much more than that," Alsemero said.

"Much more" can include both torture and damnation.

"It could not be much more," Deflores said. "There was only one thing to be confessed — the murder of Alonzo — and also she's a whore."

And also the murder of Diaphanta.

"It could not choose but follow," Alsemero said. "Oh, cunning devils! How should blind men know you from fair-faced saints?"

From within the small room, Beatrice cried, "He lies! The villain slanders me!"

"Let me go to her, sir," Deflores said.

Alsemero replied:

"Indeed, you shall go to her."

He called to Beatrice:

"Peace, crying crocodile; your sounds are heard. Silence!"

Crocodile tears are fake tears.

He then said to Deflores:

"Take your prey to you. Get you in to her, sir."

"In to" can sound like "into," in which case "Get you into her, sir" is an invitation for Deflores to have sex with Beatrice.

Deflores exited and joined Beatrice.

Alsemero said about Deflores:

"I'll be your pander now; rehearse again your scene of lust, so that you may be perfect in your roles when you shall come to act it to the black audience where howls and gnashings shall be music to you."

The black audience is in Hell.

Matthew 13:41-42 (King James Version) states:

41 The Son of man shall send forth his angels, and they shall gather out of his kingdom all things that offend, and them which do iniquity;

42 And shall cast them into a furnace of fire: there shall be wailing and gnashing of teeth."

Alsemero expected Deflores and Beatrice to have sex.

Alsemero continued:

"Clip — embrace — your adulteress freely; she is the pilot who will guide you to the Mare Mortuum, where you shall sink to bottomless fathoms."

Mare Mortuum is Latin for the Dead Sea. It was believed to be bottomless, and it can be compared to the bottomless pit of Hell.

Charon is the mythological ferryman who ferries the souls of the dead to the Land of the Dead.

Vermandero, Alibius, Isabella, Tomazo, Franciscus, and Antonio entered the scene.

"Oh, Alsemero. I have a wonder for you," Vermandero said.

"No, sir, it is I — I have a wonder for you," Alsemero said.

"I have suspicion near as proof itself about Alonzo de Piracquo's murder," Vermandero said.

"Sir, I have proof beyond suspicion about Alonzo de Piracquo's murder," Alsemero said.

Vermandero said:

"I ask you to hear me."

He pointed to Franciscus and Antonio and said:

"These two men have been disguised ever since the deed of murder was done."

"I have two other people who were more secretly disguised than your two could be, ever since the deed of murder was done," Alsemero said.

Vermandero said, "You'll hear me out. These my own servants —"

Alsemero interrupted, "Hear me out. There are those nearer than your servants who shall acquit them and prove them guiltless."

"That may be done with easy truth, sir," Franciscus said.

Tomazo said:

"How my cause is bandied — tossed back and forth — through your delays! It is urgent in blood — because I am his brother — and it calls for haste.

"Give me a brother alive or dead. If he is alive, give me a wife with him.

"If he is dead, for both him and the woman who should have been his wife, give me a recompense and retribution for murder and for adultery."

Since Beatrice should have married Alonzo, Tomazo considered any sex that Beatrice had had to be adultery.

From inside the small room, Beatrice cried, "Oh! Oh! Oh!"

Such cries can be the sound of love-making.

Alsemero said, "Hark, it is coming to you."

What is coming? Who is "you"?

Alsemero may think Deflores' penis is cumming into ('to) Beatrice.

Or he may think that Tomazo's vengeance is coming to Deflores.

From inside the small room, Deflores said, "I'll go along for company."

Whatever journey Beatrice was going to take, Deflores would go with her.

From inside the small room, Beatrice cried, "Oh! Oh!"

Such sounds can be those of something other than love-making.

Vermandero said, "What horrible sounds are these?"

"Come forth, you twins of evil," Alsemero said.

Deflores brought in Beatrice, whom he had wounded with a knife. He was supporting her as she walked.

He was her arms' supporter.

Deflores said:

"Here we are. If you have any more to say to us, speak quickly. I shall not give you the hearing otherwise. I am stout — brave and healthy — enough yet, and so, I think, is that broken rib of Mankind."

"That broken rib of Mankind" was Beatrice.

Genesis 2:21-23 (King James Version) states:

21 And the Lord God caused a deep sleep to fall upon Adam, and he slept: and he took one of his ribs, and closed up the flesh instead thereof;

22 And the rib, which the Lord God had taken from man, made he a woman, and brought her unto the man.

"An army of enemies who entered my citadel could not amaze me like this," Vermandero said. "Joanna! Beatrice Joanna!"

Beatrice said:

"Oh, do not come near me, sir; I shall defile you. I am that diseased portion of your blood that was taken from you in blood-letting for your better health. Look no more upon it but instead cast it to the ground without regard for it. Let the common sewer carry away its distinction: Let it be mixed with the contents of the sewer.

"Beneath the stars, upon yonder meteor forever hung my fate, among corruptible things. I never could pluck it from him. My loathing was prophet to the rest but never believed; my honor fell with him, and now my life."

Stars are pure and incorruptible, but meteors are impure and corruptible. Meteors are bad omens.

The meteor in Beatrice's life was Deflores. She could never pluck her fate away from him.

Beatrice continued:

"Alsemero, I am a stranger to your bed; your bed was cozened on the nuptial night, for which deception your false bride died."

"Diaphanta!" Alsemero said.

Deflores said, "Yes, and the while I coupled with your mate at barley-break; now we are left in Hell."

The game of barley-break has an area called Hell on the playing field.

While Alsemero and Diaphanta were having sex; Deflores and Beatrice were waiting — they were not having sex.

They did have lots of sex before the wedding night.

We are all there in Hell," Vermandero said. "It circumscribes and surrounds us here."

"I loved this woman in spite of her heart, which loved another man," Deflores said. "Her love I earned from Alonzo de Piracquo's murder."

"Ha, my brother's murderer!" Tomazo said.

Deflores said, "Yes, and the prize of her honor — her chastity — was my reward. I thank life for nothing except that pleasure: It was so sweet to me that I have drunk up all, leaving none behind for any man to pledge me and drink a toast to me."

"Horrid villain!" Vermandero said. "Keep life in him so he can endure further tortures."

Deflores said:

"No, I can prevent you; here's my penknife still. It is but one thread more" — he stabbed himself — "and now it is cut."

Today, penknives are very small. Not so, then. Deflores' penknife was big enough for him to use to commit murder and suicide.

His final heartstring had been cut. Now he would die.

Deflores continued:

"Make haste, Joanna, by that token to thee."

He had stabbed Beatrice Joanna, too. That was his token to her.

Deflores continued:

"Thou cannot have forgotten that token which was so recently put in your mind: I will not go and leave thee far behind. I will go with you."

He died.

Deflores had confessed but had not repented his sins.

"Forgive me, Alsemero," Beatrice said. "All of you, forgive me. It is time to die when it is a shame to live."

She died.

Beatrice had confessed and she had repented her sins.

"Oh, my name is entered now in that record where until this fatal hour it was never read!" Vermandero said.

The record was the record of critical popular opinion. Vermandero was worried about his reputation. Possibly, however, he meant the record of his good deeds and his bad deeds that was kept in Heaven.

Alsemero said:

"Let it be blotted out of the record. Let your heart lose it, and it can never look you in the face, nor tell a tale behind the back of life to your dishonor.

"Justice has so rightly and justly hit the guilty that innocence is acquitted of evil by the manifestation of the guilt of others, and the innocent may enjoy life again.

"Sir, you are aware of what truth has done; it is the best comfort that your grief can find."

Tomazo said to Vermandero, "Sir, I am satisfied; my injuries lie dead before me. I can exact no more, unless my soul were loose and could overtake those black fugitives who are fled from their corpses to endure a second vengeance in Hell; but there are wraths deeper than mine, it is to be feared, around their souls."

Alsemero said:

"What an opaque, darkened body that Moon had that last changed on us! Here's beauty changed to ugly whoredom, here servant obedience changed to a master sin — imperious murder.

"I, a supposed husband, exchanged embraces with wantonness, but that was paid before: Diaphanta died.

"Tomazo, your change has come, too, from an ignorant wrath to knowing friendship.

"Are there any more of us who have changed?"

Antonio said, "Yes, sir, I was changed, too, from a little ass as I was to a great fool as I am, and I had likely been changed to the gallows except that you know my innocence — idiocy and lack of guilt — always excuses me."

"I was changed from a little wit to be stark mad, almost for the same purpose," Franciscus said.

Isabella said to Alibius, "Your change is still to come, but you best deserve your transformation. You are a jealous coxcomb, keep schools of folly, and teach your scholars how to break your own head."

Alibius' change could possibly be to become a cuckold and grow horns on his head.

"I see all apparent, wife, and will change now into a better husband," Alibius said, "and I will never keep scholars who shall be wiser than myself."

Alsemero said to Vermandero:

"Sir, you have yet a living son's duty. Please accept it."

Alsemero was Vermandero's living son-in-law, and he would act as a dutiful son-in-law.

Alsemero continued:

"Let your sorrow, as it goes from your eye in tears, go from your heart.

"Man and his sorrow at the grave must part."

EPILOGUE

Alsemero said to you, the audience and readers:

"All that we can do to comfort one another, to stop a brother's sorrow for a brother, to dry tears from the weeping eyes of a kind father mourning the death of a child, is to no purpose; sorrow rather multiplies.

"Only your smiles have power to cause the dead to relive again, or in their rooms to give brother a new brother, to give father a child.

"If these appear, all griefs are reconciled."

All exited.

In other words: If you, the audience, applaud and approve of this play, then this play shall be acted again in rooms — in theaters — and Alonzo and Beatrice shall live again.

Also in other words: If you, the audience, applaud and approve of this play, then the actors who have been mourning on stage will become happy.

APPENDIX A: NOTES
— 1.2 —

What will result in justice: for two disputants to go into a court of law with lawyers representing each side, or for two disputants to go before a rabbi? To answer this question, Rabbi Avraham Yehoshua told this story: A wolf once killed a deer, but before it could eat the deer, a lion came along and took the deer from the wolf. Seeking justice, the wolf asked a fox to judge the dispute. The wolf claimed that he deserved the deer because he had killed it, but the lion claimed that he deserved the deer because he was the king of the jungle. The fox said that the only reasonable solution was to divide the deer, giving the wolf and the lion an equal share. However, when the fox divided the deer, it was not in equal halves, so the fox took a big bite of the larger half. Now the other half was bigger than the first half, so the fox took a big bite out of it, making the first half bigger than the second half. This continued until the fox had eaten the deer, leaving only bones for the wolf and the lion. A court of law is often like the fox: By the time the lawsuit is settled and the lawyers have received their payment, nothing is left for the disputants.

Source of Above: Retold in David Bruce's own words from Himelstein, Shmuel. *Words of Wisdom, Words of Wit*. Brooklyn, NY: Mesorah Publications, Ltd., 1993. P. 262.

— 3.3 —

The below information is the *Oxford English Dictionary* definition of "barley-break":

An old country game, varying in different parts, but somewhat resembling Prisoner's Bars, *originally played by six persons (three of each sex) in couples; one couple, being left in a middle den termed 'hell,' had to catch the others, who were allowed to separate or 'break' when hard pressed, and thus to change partners, but had when caught to take their turn as catchers. (See poetical description by Sidney in Arcadia 1. Lamon's song, and Suckling in Poems (1646) 24.) In Scotland, according to Jamieson, one person had to catch the rest of the company, each of these as taken assisting their captor.*

The below information is from the Database of Games:

A long narrow strip of ground is needed for this game divided into three spaces measuring from ten to fifty feet square. The central one of these three spaces is called the barley field. In each of the three stands a couple of players (or more as hereinafter described). The couple in the center is obliged to link arms therefore the center place is the most difficult and considered disadvantageous. The couples in the other spaces advance singly or together into the barley field trampling the barley by dancing around the field as much as they can without being caught. These couples need not link arms. When one of these is caught he must remain inactive in the barley field until his partner is also caught. The couple owning the barley field may not step beyond its limits nor may the couple being sought take refuge in the field opposite to their own. When the two are caught they become warders of the barley field changing places with the previous couple and any others who have been caught return to their own fields. The game is made interesting by not confining the effort to catching two members of the same couple in succession. Both couples in the adjoining fields should venture far into the barley taunting the couple who have linked arms by calling "Barley break." These in turn will assist their object by making feints at catching one player and turning suddenly in the opposite direction for another.

The number of players may be increased by putting three couples in the center (barley field) and two or three couples at each end.

This game is centuries old and used to be played at harvest time around the stacks in the cornfields.

Source of Above:
"Acting and Dramatic Games Barley Break." databaseofgames.com. Accessed 5 February 2023.
http://www.databaseofgames.com/physical-games/chase-and-catch/104/barley-break

The below information is from the Oxford Reference entry for "Barley-Break":

A popular chasing game, mentioned often in literary sources of the 16th to 18th centuries, played either by children or young people of both sexes. The game reconstructed by the Opies involved three mixed-sex pairs of players. One pair stood in the middle of the playing area (called 'hell'), and one pair stood at each end. The two end pairs had to change partners, without being caught by the middle pair, and the latter had to hold hands throughout. An alternative name was 'Last Couple in Hell'.

The earliest mention of the game is found in Henry's Machyn's Diary of 19 April 1557: 'The sam owre master parsun and entryd in-to helle, and ther ded at the barle breyke with alle the wyffe of the sam parryche'. Other early references include Sir Philip Sidney (Arcadia, written in 1580s), Shakespeare and Fletcher (Two Noble Kinsmen, IV. iii, 1634), and Robert Herrick (Hesperides, 1648). Other descriptions imply different ways of playing and suggest that it derives its name from originally being played in the farmyard around the stacks.

Source of Above:

"Barley-Break." Oxford Reference. Accessed 5 February 2023. https://www.oxfordreference.com/display/10.1093/oi/authority.20110803095447567

The below information is from the Wikipedia entry for "Barley-Break":

Barley-Break is an old _English_ country game frequently mentioned by the poets of the 17th and 18th centuries. It was played by three pairs, each composed of a man and a woman, who were stationed in three bases or plots, contiguous to each other. The couple occupying the middle base, called hell or prison, endeavoured to catch the other two, who, when chased, might break to avoid being caught. If one was overtaken, he and his companion were condemned to hell. From this game was taken the expression "the last couple in hell", often used in old plays.

Its use in literature usually has sexual connotations. The best known example is in _Thomas Middleton_ and _William Rowley_'s play _The Changeling_, in which an adulterer tells his _cuckold_ "I coupled with your mate at barley-break; now we are left in hell". The use of the phrase in _Thomas Morley_'s ballett "_Now Is the Month of Maying_" probably means something similar to the idiom "roll in the hay".

Source of Above:
"Barley-Break." Wikipedia. Accessed 5 February 2023. https://en.wikipedia.org/wiki/Barley-Break

$$— 3.3 —$$

Franciscus said:

"Luna is now big-bellied, and there's room for both of us to ride with Hecate. I'll drag thee up into her silver sphere, and there we'll kick the dog, and beat the bush that barks against the witches of the night."

Below are two *Oxford English Dictionary* definitions of "bush":

Anything resembling a bush; a bushy mass of foliage, feathers, etc. [1530-1648]

(A bushy growth of) pubic hair [1922-1973]

Source of Above: "Bush." *Oxford English Dictionary*.
I have to wonder if Franciscus is being bawdy.
"Big-bellied" means "pregnant."
"Ride" can mean sexual riding.
"Dog" means "male" and "bush" can mean bushy pubic hair.
"Kick" involves a vigorous movement.
"Bark" can mean the short, explosive cries of sexual enjoyment.
"Bark" can also mean "complain."
"The witches of the night" can mean deities who favor sex.

Franciscus and Lollio would be having sex with Isabella after kicking the dog Alibius. Franciscus and Lollio would be stroking Isabella's bush as she made the short, explosive cries of sexual enjoyment although she had resisted giving in to Franciscus and worshipping the goddesses of sex.

If Isabella's vulva can be likened to a Moon, Franciscus wants to be the man in her Moon.

In burlesque and other kinds of entertainment, a word can be made to sound bawdy by the inflection in the entertainer's voice.

APPENDIX B: FAIR USE

§ 107. Limitations on exclusive rights: Fair use
Release date: 2004-04-30
Notwithstanding the provisions of sections 106 and 106A, the fair use of a copyrighted work, including such use by reproduction in copies or phonorecords or by any other means specified by that section, for purposes such as criticism, comment, news reporting, teaching (including multiple copies for classroom use), scholarship, or research, is not an infringement of copyright. In determining whether the use made of a work in any particular case is a fair use the factors to be considered shall include —

(1) the purpose and character of the use, including whether such use is of a commercial nature or is for nonprofit educational purposes;

(2) the nature of the copyrighted work;

(3) the amount and substantiality of the portion used in relation to the copyrighted work as a whole; and

(4) the effect of the use upon the potential market for or value of the copyrighted work.

The fact that a work is unpublished shall not itself bar a finding of fair use if such finding is made upon consideration of all the above factors.

Source of Fair Use information:

http://www.law.cornell.edu/uscode/17/107.html

APPENDIX C: ABOUT THE AUTHOR

It was a dark and stormy night. Suddenly a cry rang out, and on a hot summer night in 1954, Josephine, wife of Carl Bruce, gave birth to a boy — me. Unfortunately, this young married couple allowed Reuben Saturday, Josephine's brother, to name their first-born. Reuben, aka "The Joker," decided that Bruce was a nice name, so he decided to name me Bruce Bruce. I have gone by my middle name — David — ever since.

Being named Bruce David Bruce hasn't been all bad. Bank tellers remember me very quickly, so I don't often have to show an ID. It can be fun in charades, also. When I was a counselor as a teenager at Camp Echoing Hills in Warsaw, Ohio, a fellow counselor gave the signs for "sounds like" and "two words," then she pointed to a bruise on her leg twice. Bruise Bruise? Oh yeah, Bruce Bruce is the answer!

Uncle Reuben, by the way, gave me a haircut when I was in kindergarten. He cut my hair short and shaved a small bald spot on the back of my head. My mother wouldn't let me go to school until the bald spot grew out again.

Of all my brothers and sisters (six in all), I am the only transplant to Athens, Ohio. I was born in Newark, Ohio, and have lived all around Southeastern Ohio. However, I moved to Athens to go to Ohio University and have never left.

At Ohio U, I never could make up my mind whether to major in English or Philosophy, so I got a bachelor's degree with a double major in both areas, then I added a Master of Arts degree in English and a Master of Arts degree in Philosophy. Yes, I have my MAMA degree.

Currently, and for a long time to come (I eat fruits and veggies), I am spending my retirement writing books such as *Nadia Comaneci: Perfect 10*, *The Funniest People in Comedy*, *Homer's* Iliad: *A Retelling in Prose*, and *William Shakespeare's* Hamlet: *A Retelling in Prose*.

If all goes well, I will publish one or two books a year for the rest of my life. (On the other hand, a good way to make God laugh is to tell Her your plans.)

By the way, my sister Brenda Kennedy writes romances such as *A New Beginning* and *Shattered Dreams*.

APPENDIX D: SOME BOOKS BY DAVID BRUCE

Retellings of a Classic Work of Literature

Arden of Faversham: *A Retelling*

Ben Jonson's The Alchemist: *A Retelling*

Ben Jonson's The Arraignment, or Poetaster: *A Retelling*

Ben Jonson's Bartholomew Fair: *A Retelling*

Ben Jonson's The Case is Altered: *A Retelling*

Ben Jonson's Catiline's Conspiracy: *A Retelling*

Ben Jonson's The Devil is an Ass: *A Retelling*

Ben Jonson's Epicene: *A Retelling*

Ben Jonson's Every Man in His Humor: *A Retelling*

Ben Jonson's Every Man Out of His Humor: *A Retelling*

Ben Jonson's The Fountain of Self-Love, or Cynthia's Revels: *A Retelling*

Ben Jonson's The Magnetic Lady, or Humors Reconciled: *A Retelling*

Ben Jonson's The New Inn, or The Light Heart: *A Retelling*

Ben Jonson's Sejanus' Fall: *A Retelling*

Ben Jonson's The Staple of News: *A Retelling*

Ben Jonson's A Tale of a Tub: *A Retelling*

Ben Jonson's Volpone, or the Fox: *A Retelling*

Christopher Marlowe's Complete Plays: Retellings

Christopher Marlowe's Dido, Queen of Carthage: *A Retelling*

Christopher Marlowe's Doctor Faustus: *Retellings of the 1604 A-Text and of the 1616 B-Text*

Christopher Marlowe's Edward II: *A Retelling*

Christopher Marlowe's The Massacre at Paris: *A Retelling*

Christopher Marlowe's The Rich Jew of Malta: *A Retelling*

Christopher Marlowe's Tamburlaine, Parts 1 and 2: *Retellings*

Dante's Divine Comedy: *A Retelling in Prose*

Dante's Inferno: *A Retelling in Prose*

Dante's Purgatory: *A Retelling in Prose*

Dante's Paradise: *A Retelling in Prose*

The Famous Victories of Henry V: *A Retelling*

From the Iliad *to the* Odyssey: *A Retelling in Prose of Quintus of Smyrna's* Posthomerica

George Chapman, Ben Jonson, and John Marston's Eastward Ho! *A Retelling*

George Peele's The Arraignment of Paris: *A Retelling*

George Peele's The Battle of Alcazar: *A Retelling*

George Peele's David and Bathsheba, and the Tragedy of Absalom: *A Retelling*

George Peele's Edward I: *A Retelling*

George Peele's The Old Wives' Tale: *A Retelling*

George-a-Greene: *A Retelling*

The History of King Leir: *A Retelling*

Homer's Iliad: *A Retelling in Prose*

Homer's Odyssey: *A Retelling in Prose*

J.W. Gent.'s The Valiant Scot: *A Retelling*

Jason and the Argonauts: A Retelling in Prose of Apollonius of Rhodes' Argonautica

John Ford: Eight Plays Translated into Modern English

John Ford's The Broken Heart: *A Retelling*

John Ford's The Fancies, Chaste and Noble: *A Retelling*

John Ford's The Lady's Trial: *A Retelling*

John Ford's The Lover's Melancholy: *A Retelling*

John Ford's Love's Sacrifice: *A Retelling*

John Ford's Perkin Warbeck: *A Retelling*

John Ford's The Queen: *A Retelling*

John Ford's 'Tis Pity She's a Whore: *A Retelling*

John Lyly's Campaspe: *A Retelling*

John Lyly's Endymion, The Man in the Moon: *A Retelling*

John Lyly's Galatea: *A Retelling*

John Lyly's Love's Metamorphosis: *A Retelling*

John Lyly's Midas: *A Retelling*

John Lyly's Mother Bombie: *A Retelling*

John Lyly's Sappho and Phao: *A Retelling*

John Lyly's The Woman in the Moon: *A Retelling*

John Webster's The White Devil: *A Retelling*

King Edward III: *A Retelling*

Mankind: *A Medieval Morality Play* (A Retelling)

Margaret Cavendish's The Unnatural Tragedy: *A Retelling*

The Merry Devil of Edmonton: *A Retelling*

The Summoning of Everyman: *A Medieval Morality Play* (A Retelling)

Robert Greene's Friar Bacon and Friar Bungay: *A Retelling*

The Taming of a Shrew: *A Retelling*

Tarlton's Jests: A Retelling

Thomas Middleton's A Chaste Maid in Cheapside: *A Retelling*

Thomas Middleton's Women Beware Women: *A Retelling*

Thomas Middleton and Thomas Dekker's The Roaring Girl: *A Retelling*

Thomas Middleton and William Rowley's The Changeling: *A Retelling*

The Trojan War and Its Aftermath: Four Ancient Epic Poems

Virgil's Aeneid: *A Retelling in Prose*

William Shakespeare's 5 Late Romances: Retellings in Prose

William Shakespeare's 10 Histories: Retellings in Prose

William Shakespeare's 11 Tragedies: Retellings in Prose

William Shakespeare's 12 Comedies: Retellings in Prose

William Shakespeare's 38 Plays: Retellings in Prose
William Shakespeare's 1 Henry IV, aka Henry IV, Part 1: A Retelling in Prose
William Shakespeare's 2 Henry IV, aka Henry IV, Part 2: A Retelling in Prose
William Shakespeare's 1 Henry VI, aka Henry VI, Part 1: A Retelling in Prose
William Shakespeare's 2 Henry VI, aka Henry VI, Part 2: A Retelling in Prose
William Shakespeare's 3 Henry VI, aka Henry VI, Part 3: A Retelling in Prose
William Shakespeare's All's Well that Ends Well: A Retelling in Prose
William Shakespeare's Antony and Cleopatra: A Retelling in Prose
William Shakespeare's As You Like It: A Retelling in Prose
William Shakespeare's The Comedy of Errors: A Retelling in Prose
William Shakespeare's Coriolanus: A Retelling in Prose
William Shakespeare's Cymbeline: A Retelling in Prose
William Shakespeare's Hamlet: A Retelling in Prose
William Shakespeare's Henry V: A Retelling in Prose
William Shakespeare's Henry VIII: A Retelling in Prose
William Shakespeare's Julius Caesar: A Retelling in Prose
William Shakespeare's King John: A Retelling in Prose
William Shakespeare's King Lear: A Retelling in Prose
William Shakespeare's Love's Labor's Lost: A Retelling in Prose
William Shakespeare's Macbeth: A Retelling in Prose
William Shakespeare's Measure for Measure: A Retelling in Prose
William Shakespeare's The Merchant of Venice: A Retelling in Prose
William Shakespeare's The Merry Wives of Windsor: A Retelling in Prose
William Shakespeare's A Midsummer Night's Dream: A Retelling in Prose
William Shakespeare's Much Ado About Nothing: A Retelling in Prose
William Shakespeare's Othello: A Retelling in Prose
William Shakespeare's Pericles, Prince of Tyre: A Retelling in Prose
William Shakespeare's Richard II: A Retelling in Prose
William Shakespeare's Richard III: A Retelling in Prose
William Shakespeare's Romeo and Juliet: A Retelling in Prose
William Shakespeare's The Taming of the Shrew: A Retelling in Prose
William Shakespeare's The Tempest: A Retelling in Prose
William Shakespeare's Timon of Athens: A Retelling in Prose
William Shakespeare's Titus Andronicus: A Retelling in Prose
William Shakespeare's Troilus and Cressida: A Retelling in Prose
William Shakespeare's Twelfth Night: A Retelling in Prose
William Shakespeare's The Two Gentlemen of Verona: A Retelling in Prose
William Shakespeare's The Two Noble Kinsmen: A Retelling in Prose
William Shakespeare's The Winter's Tale: A Retelling in Prose